EXIT 13

THE SPACES IN BETWEEN

BY JAMES PRELLER

EXIT 13

THE SPACES IN BETWEEN

BY JAMES PRELLER

Scholastic Inc.

© 2023 Scholastic Inc.

All rights reserved. Published by Scholastic Inc., *Publishers since 1920.*
SCHOLASTIC and associated logos are trademarks and/or registered trademarks of Scholastic Inc. The publisher does not have any control over and does not assume any responsibility for author or third-party websites or their content.

No part of this publication may be reproduced, stored in a retrieval system, or transmitted in any form or by any means, electronic, mechanical, photocopying, recording, or otherwise, without written permission of the publisher. For information regarding permission, write to Scholastic Inc., Attention: Permissions Department, 557 Broadway, New York, NY 10012.

This book is a work of fiction. Names, characters, places, and incidents are either the product of the author's imagination or are used fictitiously, and any resemblance to actual persons, living or dead, business establishments, events, or locales is entirely coincidental.

ISBN 978-1-338-81045-5

10 9 8 7 6 5 4 3 2 1   23 24 25 26 27

Printed in the U.S.A.   37

First edition 2023

This book is dedicated to Debra Dorfman and Elizabeth Bennett. Thank you for believing in me.

—J.P.

ONE

IN THE BRIGHT, early morning, Willow, Ash, and Mrs. McGinn gathered outside their rooms at Exit 13 Motel. Mr. McGinn methodically packed the car for today's trip. Daisy, the family dog, was especially excited—she was always up for a ride in the car, windows down, preferably.

"Sorry, Daisy," Mr. McGinn said. "It's just me this time."

Willow, thirteen, watched with her arms crossed. She would normally crack a joke at a moment like this. A snarky aside or something. But nothing the least bit funny came to mind. She glanced sideways at her

1

brother, Ash. He looked like a coiled spring, jittery and nervous, lips knit together in a frown. Was it possible that Ash was the most intense eleven-year-old on the planet? Willow gave it a maybe.

For the past four days, Mr. McGinn had taken off on similar trips. And though each journey ended in bitter disappointment, Mrs. McGinn stood beside her husband. She glowed with positive vibes.

Mr. McGinn checked his list twice, just like Santa before harnessing the reindeer: "Okay, hmmm. Flashlight, extra batteries, emergency mylar thermal blanket, backpack, first aid kit, maps, compass, utility knife, lighter, waterproof matches, axe, tire repair kit, food supplies, jumper cables, hiking boots, whistle, two dozen bottles of water, spare clothes, cash, cell phone, duct tape . . ."

He looked to his wife. "Duct tape, honey?"

"It's in the trunk," Mrs. McGinn answered.

Willow finally spoke up. "Dad, do you have to go through with this? You know how it's going to end."

"Yes, I do know," Mr. McGinn told his daughter. "I am going to succeed. I am going to find a way out of here, once and for all. Because I am your father—and that's what fathers do."

Willow shut her mouth. Her heart clenched like a fist. She didn't tell her father that this trip was surely going to be like all the others. He would return again, in less than a minute, a failure. And with each return, her father looked a little more broken, a little more defeated.

There was no escape from Exit 13.

"Come on, bring it in," Mr. McGinn said, holding his arms out. The family huddled in a group hug. Even Daisy pressed against their legs. "You don't have to do this," Mrs. McGinn reminded her husband. "Maybe it's best to rest a few days."

"Isn't this the definition of insanity?" Ash added. "To do the same thing over and over again, and expect a different result?"

"But I'm not doing the same thing, son," Mr. McGinn replied. "I've learned from each failure. I'm more prepared this time."

You had to give him credit. Deckland Seaver McGinn had an almost inexhaustible supply of hope. So Mr. McGinn got in the car, gently tapped the horn, and pulled out of the parking lot.

A crow cawed and landed on the roof of the motel.

A cloud passed in front of the sun.

Daisy scratched behind her ear.

Full of dread and expectation, Willow counted silently to herself: *seven, eight, nine . . .*

Mr. McGinn pulled back into the same parking space.

He was back in no time at all.

And he looked terrible. Exhausted with dark circles under his eyes. His face thick with stubble. There was a bruise over his right eye. He climbed out of the car, shoulders stooped, pants muddied and torn. "Dad, are you okay?"

Mr. McGinn could not bring himself to look anyone in the eye. He wearily checked his watch. "I'm sorry," he said. "I'm so sorry."

His wife went to his side. She brushed a hand through his hair. "You are back with us, that's the important thing. Our family is together. That's all that matters."

"I've been gone one hundred and fifty-three hours," he said in a hoarse voice. He coughed. "Six and a half days. When the fog rolled in, I pulled over and tried bushwhacking through the forest. It rained and rained.

And every time I came back to the same place. Over and over again. No matter how hard I tried . . ."

"Oh, sweetie. Come inside. You need to lie down."

He wheezed, eyes downcast.

"Maybe Kristoff is right," Willow volunteered, trying to be helpful. "We're trapped in some weird rift in time and space. Like the fabric of the universe is torn. Kristoff says—"

"I'm tired of hearing about Kristoff," Mr. McGinn snapped. "As far as I'm concerned, he's part of this. I don't trust him, Willow, and I don't want you spending time with that boy."

"Honey," Mrs. McGinn said in a soothing voice. "This is hard on everyone. Come inside for a hot shower. It sounds like you've caught a cold."

The door to room 16 opened and closed.

Willow and Ash and Daisy stood outside.

"He couldn't even look at us," Ash said.

The crow flew away, black wings beating ceaselessly against the sky.

TWO

ROOM FIFTEEN, two twin beds separated by six feet. A shared nightstand between them, a television on a large dresser across the room, exactly one chair, and a bathroom. It wasn't Caesars Palace. It wasn't even the Red Roof Inn. But for Willow and Ash, it was home for the foreseeable future. They sat on their beds facing each other, knees not quite touching.

Willow scratched Daisy behind the ears. She asked her brother, "Seriously, do you think we'll ever get out of here?"

"I don't know."

"It kills me to see Dad this way," Willow said.

"Dad will be fine. You know what he's like," Ash said. "He won't give up."

"And Mom? She acts like we should accept it."

Ash shrugged. "Maybe she's right. Mom is more practical. Maybe this is our life now."

Willow looked around at the room. "Great, I share a bedroom with my little brother—and my father doesn't want to me to talk to the only cute guy around."

"Kristoff is a little old for you, don't you think?"

"He's fifteen."

Ash shook his head. "My guess is he's trapped here just like us—but maybe for a lot longer."

Willow groaned.

"Dad was gone for what? One minute?" Ash continued. "But to him it was almost a week. Time here stretches like a rubber band. If Kristoff has been here for years, how long is that in real time?"

"Terrific, my vampire hottie is two hundred and eighty-seven years old," Willow joked. "He still has great hair."

They both laughed. What else could they do?

"You know," Willow said. "Kristoff once said something to me. I was asking about the Whispering

Pines. How it must be hard for him, living here with only his mother, to watch so many people come and go."

"Yeah, and what did he say?"

"Nothing, really," Willow admitted. "He never reveals much. It was more just a vibe I got. Like he's been lonely for a long, long time."

Ash leaned forward and lowered his voice to a whisper. "You know that you can't listen to Dad. We need to learn more about Kristoff. If we are ever going to get out of this place, we're going to have to learn their secrets. What's up with his mother? Why do we never see her?"

Willow nodded.

Ash invited Daisy up on the bed. The dog rolled over, offering up her warm belly. "Willow, can you promise to keep a secret?"

"Of course, LB." She sometimes called him that— short for Little Brother. The nickname wouldn't last much longer. Ash was growing up fast.

"The other night while you were sleeping, I followed the dire wolf to the door without a number, between rooms seven and eight. I'm telling you, the wolf led me there. It kept looking over its shoulder. The door to the room was unlocked. So I went inside—"

"Wait, you followed the wolf? When was this?"

Ash shrugged. "I don't know. Time is so weird in this place. It was before we tried to check out the first time."

"So, like, five days ago?" Willow said. "And you never told me?"

"Anyway," Ash said, ignoring the question, "it wasn't anything like an ordinary motel room. It was set up like a reading area. With a stuffed chair and old-fashioned lamp and a big bookshelf against the wall. I found a weird book, Will. It was called *The Book of Liminal Spaces*. I know it was important. Like it was left there for me."

"Left there for you?" Willow repeated doubtfully.

Ash nodded. He was deadly serious. "I looked up liminal spaces in the dictionary. They are in-between places, Willow. A crossing-over space. Like a hallway that connects two rooms."

Willow leaned back and crossed her arms. "So you are telling me that you followed a giant wolf into a room and found a book that someone left for you?"

Ash could see that Willow didn't believe him. He

should have known better. He decided that he'd refrain from telling her about turning invisible . . . camouflaging himself like a chameleon. Or the secret hatch he'd discovered in the wardrobe. She wasn't ready to hear it. "Forget it," he grumbled.

"No, no, I'm sorry," Willow said. "I mean, sure, it's totally bananas. All of it. Everything about this place. We're trapped in a dumpy motel, Ash. We can't escape. So, I mean, sure, I'll believe anything at this point. Where's the book now?"

"Something happened—I got scared—and I left it in the room," Ash said. "I have a feeling that book can teach us how this place works. We've got to get it back."

"You mean, like . . . sneak in and steal it?"

"I prefer *borrow it*," Ash said, "but yeah, something like that."

Willow smiled. "It's not only a motel, it's a library, too. We just want to borrow a book!"

THREE

FIRST THINGS FIRST: Daisy needed a walk. Ash clipped the leash to her collar and began what had become their regular loop around the motel. The door to room 15 opened to a view of a paved parking lot, rectangular in shape, with designated spaces for forty-eight vehicles. Currently, it held a total of five parked cars. Loose gravel and small potholes reinforced the impression that it had been some time since any upkeep had been made. Beyond the pavement, there was a grassy area that sloped down to tangled underbrush and scrawny trees. Daisy enjoyed nosing around there. Sometimes there were rabbits. A driveway to the left wound down to the main road below (the motel itself was perched on an overlook). There was a surprisingly vibrant garden bursting with color; this was the domain of Mr. Do, the all-purpose "fixer upper" employed by the motel. He labored in the garden now. The old Korean man stood straight and watched—hands on hips, straw hat atop his head—as Ash progressed across the dry, sunbaked lawn. Mr. Do did not smile or wave. He gave a slight head bow of recognition. Ash lifted his chin in reply. He noted the ring of old-fashioned keys attached to Mr. Do's belt loop. Surely one of those would open the secrets of the Unnumbered Room. But how to acquire them? It was a riddle to solve.

Ash continued clockwise to the right—past the empty pool—beyond the "social area" of picnic tables and a faded shuffleboard court. Beside that, a modest pavilion and picnic area, complete with an outdoor barbecue. The McGinns grilled there on most nights.

They made the turn past the vending machines and around to the back side of the motel. That's where the Whispering Pines began. The expanse of forest stretched out for miles. It was state land, left undeveloped. No roads, no houses, nothing at all. Just gaping wilderness.

From the day the McGinns arrived, Ash and Willow were warned to stay out of the woods—by Kristoff and Mr. Do. It was dangerous, a person could get lost, turned around in the forest, and wander off never to be found. Or so they said.

Every time Ash made that turn, he felt the tension in his neck. Like he was standing on a train track. He couldn't see the locomotive in the distance, but he felt its vibration in the steel rails. That big train was on its way.

A feeling that said: *I'm not here yet, but I'm coming.*

His breath grew shallow; Ash couldn't seem to get quite enough oxygen in his lungs. Even Daisy sensed it, or smelled it in that mystical way dogs possess. Able to follow invisible trails. Daisy stayed close to his side, the leash gone limp.

At Exit 13 Motel, there were things Ash saw, things he remembered, and things, perhaps, he only imagined. He wasn't sure which was which anymore. It had been that way for all his life. But here, in this place, it had gotten much worse. For example, those rustling branches in the understory. It could have been the wind. Or two squirrels at play, climbing and leaping off branches, a couple of bushy-tailed acrobats on a summer morning. But today, the movement was caused by the great wolf. Usually Ash only felt its eyes—its red eyes—peering at him from the forest dark.

The wolf stepped out into the open, revealing its muzzle with its ragged scar, black-tipped ears, and huge head. The wolf's stare drilled down to Ash's core. It was only fifty feet away.

Daisy whimpered and pulled as far as the leash allowed.

"Shhhh, shhhh," Ash shushed. "It's all right. That wolf won't hurt us."

Which was a lie that Ash told himself. It's fine, we're fine, everything's fine . . . even when a ghost wolf gives us the hard, lean, hungry stare. Had to be a ghost, right? It couldn't be a *real* wolf, Ash reasoned. He'd read up on it. Wolves weren't active in these parts, and even if they were—because anything was possible—no living wolf could ever be *that* big.

Its front legs were powerful and its broad chest was thrust forward. A forbidding animal.

"What do you want, wolf?" Ash asked. "Why do you follow me every day?"

14

Hearing this, the wolf lowered its head, flicked its bushy tail, and retreated into the woods.

Gone—if it was ever there in the first place.

What was real and what was only imagined? Ash couldn't tell anymore. He wondered if it even mattered. The wind rustled through the pines. Or was it a whispering voice? Only the murmur of needles meeting air, that was all, nothing else. Calling to him, "Asssshhh, Assssshhh."

The sticker bushes weren't tugging at his sleeve, the tangle of thorns weren't tearing at his skin. The forest wasn't luring him into the deep, dark places.

It only felt that way.

Ash once wandered deep into these same woods and returned carrying a cat. A rescue cat; a very strange, otherworldly creature. Willow told him to give it to Justice, a girl who had been staying at the motel. And so he did. What did Justice name it? Ash tried to remember. *Train*, that was it. He wondered if maybe there were more lost animals that needed saving. Or was he the one in need of salvation?

As if waking from a dream, Ash blinked, shook his head, and looked around. He found himself standing at the exact spot where the wolf once stood. His feet had taken him here. An icy gust of wind passed through him. Like a ghost train entering a tunnel. He heard a cry—it was Daisy, whining, pulling on the leash—and so Ash backed slowly away.

Daisy was right.

He felt it, too.

There was something dangerous in that forest.

FOUR

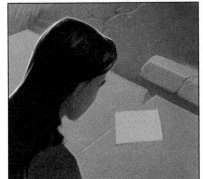

1st Annual
UFO FEST!

UFO Experts!
Vendor Booths & Workshops!
Cosmic Costume Contest!
Abduction Survivors Tell Their Stories!
Games, Fun, & More!

THEY ARE OUT THERE!

FIVE

THE OFFICE WAS CROWDED—WILLOW had never seen that many guests at the motel. One woman with a high forehead and smooth brown skin stood impatiently, tapping fingernails on the counter. *Fuudddup, fuudddup, fuuddup.* Her nails sounded like heavy-booted soldiers marching through muddy streets. Three other people milled around, waiting their turn. They all had a definite look to them, as if they had just arrived from a camping trip on Mars. One guy, maybe thirty, wore a baseball cap backward. He had a backpack slung over his shoulder. A green alien figure dangled from a key chain. He was wearing pajama bottoms and Crocs.

A hairy dude with an extreme beard was dressed in baggy shorts and a denim jacket. He looked strong and powerful. A flying saucer was hand-painted on the back of the jacket, floating above the word BELIEVE.

The telephone rang, and rang, and rang.

Kristoff sat typing at the keyboard, frowning at the computer monitor. He vibrated stress.

"When will my room be available?" the woman at the counter asked. "We'd like to drop off our things and get back to the convention hall. Opening ceremonies begin at 3:00."

A man shook his head. He groaned to another. "We're going to miss Dr. Zappa's talk on cosmic debris."

"Can we *please* hurry it up?" bleated the alien-dangling-from-a-key-chain-pajama-bottom-wearing guy.

The phone continued to ring.

Kristoff ran a hand through his hair. It looked to Willow like he might want to rip it out. His hair *and* the phone.

"Are you the only one who works here?" another voice wondered aloud. "This is taking forever."

"My apologies," Kristoff answered. "I didn't expect this on a Thursday—"

Briiiinnnngggg, briiiinnnngggg, the phone insisted.

Willow stepped forward to pick up the receiver. "Exit 13 Motel, how may I help you?"

Kristoff looked at her in surprise and, she saw, a wave of relief. He indicated a space for her behind the counter. A message pad and pen.

"Thank you for your interest. Please hold while I check on availability." Willow cupped her palm over the receiver. "Anything?"

Kristoff replied, "Counting reservations and all these walk-ins, we're booked solid for at least the next four nights. No vacancies until Monday."

Willow politely explained that there were no rooms available. She was about to suggest that they might call back another time when, *click,* the caller hung up without so much as a thank-you.

Ugh, some people, Willow grumbled to herself.

Kristoff handed a key over to the fingernail-tapping woman (whose braided extensions, Willow noted, were beyond cool).

The door opened and somebody barked, "Still need

that roll-away cot for room eleven! Today, if possible."

Kristoff quietly fumed.

"I can get it," Willow offered.

Kristoff looked at her. "Yeah, okay, here." He snatched a spare set of keys off a wall hook and tossed them in her direction. "The square one is a master. It opens every room. Spare cots and linens are in the supply room around back."

"On it," Willow replied. She thumbed the keys. Meanwhile, her mind mulled over Kristoff's words. *A master key that opens every room.* Bingo! She turned to the man at the door. "Sir, I'll happily wheel that cot to your room before you can count to five hundred thousand bananas."

The man looked at her blankly.

Willow smiled. "Give me five minutes."

Half an hour later, the office was empty. Willow was pleased to see that the light to the NO VACANCY sign actually worked. Not many things around the motel did. Kristoff sat collapsed in a chair, a stunned expression on his face. "That was intense. I'm not used to dealing with that many guests at once."

"What was that all about?" Willow asked.

"There's some big UFO festival in town. The Star Hotel on Main Street double-booked people by accident and now everybody's scrambling to find accommodations—and they are all angry. I had to turn customers away."

The phone rang.

Kristoff looked at it wearily.

"Exit 13 Motel," Willow answered in her sunniest voice. "How may we help you?"

Ten minutes and three brief phone calls later—seriously, people were stressed out!—Willow left the office with a part-time job. "Just to get us through this rough patch," Kristoff clarified. "It's not permanent."

"Sure thing!" Willow said, grinning happily. "Besides, my father says we're leaving any day now . . . *ha, ha, ha.*"

Kristoff chuckled at Willow's dark humor.

On the way back to her room, Willow felt a lump in her front pocket. *Oh yes*, she had "accidentally forgotten" to return the spare keys. How very clever. Willow wondered how long it would take Kristoff to notice they were missing.

SIX

MR. MCGINN WASN'T HIS USUAL cheerful self during dinner, so their mother enlisted the children in a game of cards. "It makes your father happy when we're all together," she confided. They gathered around the picnic table at evening's last light, playing a round of Oh, Well. It was a trick-taking card game, sometimes called Nomination Whist, where the object was to take the exact number of tricks bid. A game of skill and luck that the McGinns competed at with surprising ferocity. Though each family member was capable of winning at any time, Mom was recognized as the reigning champ. "I will destroy you all without mercy" was the kind of thing she said while chomping on a carrot stick. Willow always kept score.

Ash's thoughts drifted from the game. Later that night, he planned to sneak into the Unnumbered Room. Willow had totally come through with the master key. But first, he needed everyone at the motel to go to sleep. It was important that no one saw him enter or exit the room.

"I noticed that the family from room four drove away today," Willow commented.

Mr. McGinn peered over his fan of cards. "And?"

"And nothing," Willow answered. "They never came back."

"I guess they got out," Mrs. McGinn commented. "Most people seem to."

"So it's us," Ash said. "The motel wants us."

"You actually think the building wants us?" Willow scoffed.

No one replied. The thought just hung there like a sad, half-inflated birthday balloon.

"I wonder what would happen," mused Mr. McGinn, "if I hid in the trunk. What do you think, honey? Would that work? Then I could get help."

His wife didn't answer. She was shuffling the cards, not thrilled with the conversation. "Let's just be here now," she bristled. "We're all together, playing cards. Let's try to enjoy that."

Ash noticed a car pull up with dark-tinted windows. A bald, trim man stepped out. He wore a dark suit and mirrored sunglasses, which was strange for this time of night. It was dusk and the motel's floodlights weren't exactly bright. The man wheeled a large travel bag across the asphalt. He glanced toward the picnic area and his gaze lingered on Ash—for one beat too long. Something happened with the man's mouth. His lips neither smiled nor frowned. They *grimaced* for a flickering instant. As if they had tasted something he didn't like. A bitter flavor.

Ash felt his nerve endings jangle.

Warning bells went off inside his brain.

Something about that guy wasn't right.

"Ash? It's your move," Mrs. McGinn said.

Ash studied his hand. The cards he'd been dealt. He threw down the king of hearts and hoped that no one had an ace up their sleeve.

"So, um," Willow began. "I got a job today."

That's how she broke the news. Over a game of chance. Before her parents could object, Willow explained about the day's rush of wacky new guests, spillovers from the UFO Fest. "Kristoff was totally overwhelmed and—"

"Willow, I told you to stay away from that boy," her father said.

"Yeah, I remember," Willow shot back. "But look around, Dad. Where am I supposed to go? What am I supposed to do? I can't stay locked up in my room all day."

Willow's mother reached out, placing a gentle hand on Willow's forearm. "Tell us more," she said in a quiet voice, "about the job itself."

Becalmed, Willow detailed how she'd be answering phones, making coffee, helping clean the rooms, and watching the office when Kristoff had to attend to other things. She shrugged. "I don't know, honestly. Just kind of help out in general. It's just for the next few days."

Because it was an unwritten rule that siblings must stick together against their parents at all costs, Ash quickly chimed in with "I think it's awesome."

"I don't like it," Mr. McGinn pronounced.

"But, honey. Think about it. It might be good for Will. And I do worry about that boy," Mrs. McGinn sympathized. "He seems all alone. A sick mother who we still haven't seen? What's going on there? Willow's just trying to be kind."

Mr. McGinn exhaled loudly and tossed his remaining cards on the table. "So I'm the bad guy now? I don't want my only daughter to be *kind*? Is that it? Well, I can see that I've been outvoted." He stood and stepped away from the table. "Deal me out. I'm done for the night."

"Dad, don't be like—"

"Leave your father be," Willow's mother said. She watched her husband walk away. Shoulders slumped, head down. Defeated again. "He'll be all right. He's just worried about us. Frightened about what's been happening."

"What about you, Mom? Are you afraid?" Ash asked.

"I'm trying hard not to think about it," she answered. "Fear never helps anyone get to where they need to go."

SEVEN

WILLOW HAD PROMISED that she would wait up with Ash. But by the time midnight rolled around, and then 1:00 a.m., she was fully zonked and snoring. Willow usually slept on her back, mouth open, arms extended, and at least one leg sticking out from beneath the covers. Ash snapped a photo, because that's what brothers do. It might be useful as blackmail down the road.

He peeked through the blinds. There was no sure way to tell if the coast was clear without stepping outside. He'd tested it twice already. Both times the bald, goateed man sat in a chair outside room 6. A long, sharp knife glistened in his hand as he carved a block of wood. *Whittling*, Ash thought; funny, the man didn't seem like the crafty type. Both times the man turned his head to look. No greeting, no recognition; just a hard, cold stare. The first time, Ash was prepared. He immediately turned right and loped to the vending machines at the side of the building. Slotted in the coins and purchased peanut M&M's. The second time, at 12:30, Ash did a big stretch, looked up at the moon, and yawned loudly. He whispered to Daisy and walked her out to the nearest patch of grass. Just a regular sleepy kid letting his dog out to pee. Nothing to see here, nothing at all.

The guy seemed to be waiting on something.

Or keeping guard.

Still bent over his block of wood, but now wearing a bright orange Band-Aid on an index finger. Maybe not so good with that knife after all.

Ash laid down for a short rest. His eyes shot open at 2:46 a.m., according to the digital clock on the night table. Daisy watched without lifting her head, aware of the boy's every movement. Ash rinsed his face in the bathroom. He took a deep breath, focused his thoughts, and once again stepped out the front door.

There was no one around.

Ash listened, unmoving.

Not a sound, not a footfall.

No sign of the wolf, either.

He walked on silent feet until he came to the Unnumbered Door between rooms 7 and 8. He took the master key from his pocket. Made a wish. Slid it into the lock. And turned.

Click. The door opened.

Ash made one last furtive look up and down the long cement walkway. Nothing. No one. He pushed open the door and shut it behind him.

Darkness.

He had forgotten the flashlight.

Ash waited, his back to the closed door, body trembling. He listened for the faintest sounds—and heard only his own heartbeat, the blood rumbling through his veins. And slowly something strange happened—but it was so gradual, so glacial, that Ash didn't realize it at first.

Then all at once, he knew.

I can see.

I can see in the dark.

How weird was that? It was as if he had mysteriously developed night vision. *Pretty cool.*

The room was exactly as Ash remembered.

It smelled damp, musty.

A feral animal scent.

Of blood and meat and crushed bones.

Of nights bedding down in the damp earth, warmed by leaves and forest dross and protected under the arms of the great trees.

This was, Ash sensed, the lair of the wolf.

Even though that made no sense at all.

(Trapped at Exit 13 Motel, Ash was slowly learning to let go of "things making sense.")

Heavy curtains had been pulled across the window. Floor-to-ceiling bookshelves took up the full opposite wall, packed with old books. A large wooden wardrobe leaned against the perpendicular wall to his left. This was the wall shared with room 8. The wardrobe itself was a puzzle. It was too big for this space; it didn't fit, didn't make sense for the room. And yet here it was. In the corner to Ash's right, there was a heavy, stuffed chair and a freestanding lamp.

There was a small round table by the chair. A glass of water.

And the book he had come for: *The Book of Liminal Spaces*.

The book was open, facedown, spine up. Ash picked it up. Sniffed it. The odor of wolf. The pages had been opened to a chapter titled "Seeing in the Dark."

Ash methodically repeated what he had done in his previous visit. He opened the wardrobe door. A dowel with empty clothes hangers. A water bowl—oddly—on the floor. Ash shut the door and turned his attention to the bookcase to his right. A leaping wolf was carved into the wood. He ran his fingers over it: snout, ears, limbs, claws. The wardrobe door popped open a few inches, as if a lock unclasped.

An invitation from beyond.

He pulled the door open all the way. This time, the wardrobe was empty except for a thick, metal ring on the floor. A white nylon cord was attached to it. The boy hesitated in the stillness. He pulled open the hatch.

EIGHT

THE OPEN HATCH revealed a metal ladder attached to the side of a long, narrow hole. Big enough for one body to climb down into a darkness—a pitch that even Ash's keen sight could not penetrate. He placed his hand above the hole. A draft met his outstretched fingers. A chill shivered his spine. *What was down there? Where did the tunnel lead? Why was it here?* This late at night, there was no way Ash was going down there to explore. Not today. And not alone. He wasn't ready to face whatever might be down there.

He gently closed the hatch, making sure not to cause a sound. Ash stood and shut the wardrobe door.

Out of curiosity, he opened it again. The closet had transformed back: a dowel, clothes hangers, shelves, a ceramic water bowl on the floor. Neat trick. He wondered how it worked. With the book tight in his hand, Ash paused at the main doorway. If he removed the book from the room, they would know—whoever "they" were. And maybe that's ultimately why he decided to take it. Not only for the magic the book seemed to contain. But also because maybe that was part of the plan.

For Ash to find the book.

For Ash to read it, *absorb* it.

Was that the motel's purpose all along?

Was it crazy to think that way? That the building had intentions, desires, and plans? Ash opened the room door a crack and put his ear to it, hoping against hope that no one was around.

Ash paused, ears straining against the silence. He heard nothing except for his own body—his own bated breath—in the quiet. And beyond, in the distance, the woods played their own eerie nighttime symphony. Tree frogs croaked. The leathery wings of bats flapped against the still night air. Foxes cried like abandoned infants. Coyotes howled. Barn owls screeched and rodents perished with muffled gasps.

Other than all that? Silence.

He was alone.

Or so he thought.

Ash headed stealthily to his room, mission accomplished.

Then he heard it.

A clink, a chair scraping on cement.

He glanced toward the pool area. The was no water in the pool, but lounge chairs still outlined the perimeter. It was dark. The overhead lights had automatically shut off during the night. Ash thought maybe he could make out a shape, a shadow in the black.

Somebody there.

Had he been seen?

Huh?

LATE NIGHT, EH?

WHAT YOU BEEN UP TO, BRO?

THE WHISPER CARRIED ACROSS EMPTY SPACE. LAUGHTER ROLLED IN LIKE THE MORNING SURF.

Hee-hee, hee-haw, hee-hee.

NINE

IF ONLY HER MOTHER could see her now.

Willow the slob.

Willow the mess.

Willow the hopeless.

Willow the teenager with clothes scattered everywhere, bed unmade. Last week's half-eaten cereal in a bowl on the floor, hardened into cement.

Now she was changing the bedsheets in room 4. Scrubbing the toilet. Spraying down the bathroom with disinfectant. Running a vacuum over the rug. All the things a housekeeper does to make the room presentable. A family of three was scheduled to check in that afternoon. Willow stood, stretched her back, and wiped her brow. Housekeeping was hard, physical work. At least the pay was lousy.

The funny thing was, Willow didn't mind. The work felt useful, productive. She wore earbuds and moved to the music. It gave her time to think. Willow wondered, *Does this make me a maid? Do people even use that word anymore—or is that sexist?*

A female flight attendant used to be called a stewardess. A firefighter was called a fireman. A meteorologist was a weatherman. And according to Willow's mother, who *knew things*, a woman who wrote a book was once called an authoress. Times change. Hopefully for the better. Willow preferred *housekeeper* to *cleaning lady*. A small victory over the language. Down with the patriarchy!

The cell dinged and Willow reached for her phone. At the motel, she only received texts from her family and, earlier today, just once so far, a message from Kristoff: "Ice bucket to room nine." It didn't include a smiley emoji. Not Kristoff's style. No one from "outside" ever got through. Willow was unable to reach any of her friends back home. Kristoff called it a "Dead

Zone." She guessed he was right. Whatever rules worked out in the real world, they didn't apply to Exit 13 Motel. Willow might as well have existed on a different planet.

But still, with every ding, she hoped.

Today's message read:

> **Unlisted: There is more power here than you realize.**
> **It is ancient and restless.**

Okay, yeah, that was weird. Willow replied:

> **Willow: Who is this?**

The message box showed three animated dots to indicate that someone was typing a reply. But no message came. Willow frowned, annoyed. She slipped the phone into her back pocket.

Was it from Ash? Goofing on her? Probably, right? But was he tech savvy enough to figure out how to send anonymous text messages? Doubtful. Her parents? Forget it. Her father could barely type a message.

"I have fat thumbs like sausages!" he complained. "Why can't people just talk anymore?"

So who could it have been? Kristoff?

She kept working her way down the row of rooms. Five was a mess, a heap of towels on the bathroom floor, garbage can overflowing with pizza boxes, chicken wings, and empty liter bottles of Coke.

She knocked on room 6, waited, and knocked again. Just as she was about to turn the master key, the door opened about twelve inches. A scowling bald man with mirrored sunglasses and a precisely trimmed goatee stared at her. "What?"

"Housekeeping," Willow replied.

(She eyed her reflection in the man's sunglasses. Willow McGinn, professional housekeeper!)

"Not needed," he replied.

"Oh, sure," Willow said. "Do you want me to empty your garbage or—"

"No."

"I have some fresh towels if you'd like—"

The door opened wider. The man stood in suit pants and a crisp white undershirt (except for the mustard stain). There was also a small dab of shaving cream on his right earlobe. He had dark circles under his eyes. He held out a hand impatiently.

Willow handed over the stack of fresh and neatly folded towels. She glanced over the man's shoulder. He had set up a bunch of computer monitors on the dresser. One of them was huge, television-sized. Papers and folders were scattered on the bed. It looked like a control center.

"Is that it?" the man asked. He glanced back over his shoulder and started to pull the door closed.

"Oh, um, yeah, I mean, no!" Willow stammered. She pointed into the room. "Should I take away the old towels?"

A sound came out of the man's mouth. A grunt of annoyance. "What I want," he said in clipped tones, "is for this *thing* that we're doing here—this interruption— to end. I would rather *not* be wasting my time talking to a maid about dirty towels. How old are you, any- way? Twelve?"

"I'm sixteen," Willow lied.

"Uh-huh," the man grunted.

Willow took a half step back. She felt irritated by this guy's tough guy act. She waggled her fingers by her ears. "You might want to—"

"What?" he said.

"You know, with the towel."

"What are you talking about?" the man demanded.

Willow pointed and, with an air of perfect innocence, said: "You have shaving cream on your ear."

(Man, she so enjoyed saying that!)

A flicker of discomfort crossed the man's face. For that one second, he was just a little boy. Then he slammed the door in Willow's face.

What a complete and total doofus.

(The sunglasses were cool, though.)

Willow rolled the cart to the next door. His voice called behind her, "Hey, you, girl!"

The Complete and Total Doofus stood leaning out the door, one foot on the walkway, one hand on the knob.

Willow only half turned. She would hate to lose her job on the first day. *"Oh, the guy in room six? Sorry, Kristoff, but I speared him in the chest with a broom handle. Was that not good housekeeping?"*

"Last night," he said. "I heard sounds at my bathroom window. Scratches. Growls. Does this dump

45

have wild dogs running around? You should get animal control out here."

Willow smiled. "Dogs? No, not that I know about. Warthogs, yeah, they're a problem."

The man raised an eyebrow.

"And wombats," Willow said. "Just warthogs and wombats, mostly. And walruses, but only in winter."

"You think you're funny?"

Willow grinned. "I guess not?"

"No," he replied.

"At least I tried," Willow said. "I'll be sure to share your concerns with my manager."

The man turned and went back inside without another word.

Her phone dinged again:

Unlisted: Beware of the man in room six.
Willow: No kidding!

After a pause, she typed again:

Willow: Who are you?

Willow didn't expect an answer. But in a few moments, one arrived.

Unlisted: A.F.

At least now the anonymous texter had a name. Or initials, anyway. Totally not at all helpful. What a day. Willow looked down the long row of rooms. The parking lot had mostly emptied out. All the guests, she guessed, were in town for the convention. It made her think about the man in room 6. *What was he doing here? And why did she need to beware of him?*

TEN

ASH HAD COME to think of it as Mr. Do's Magic Garden. There was something serene about the place. The garden wasn't very large, but it was cared for meticulously. Everything in its place. Orderly and neat. A white gravel path wound through flowers and plants of every color and variety, centered around a koi pond complete with orange fish and trickling waterfall. Best of all, Ash liked sitting on the stone bench. In the morning, the sun would tumble into his lap; by late afternoon, it would warm his back and shoulders. When a boy shared one lousy room with his sister, it was important to get outside.

On this day, Ash brought a book. Not just any book, but *the book*. Daisy lay sprawled by his feet, snoozing in the afternoon sun. Mr. Do worked quietly, digging in the dirt.

In a certain respect, Ash read in the same way that Mr. Do gardened. Slowly, patiently. It wasn't the type of book that you blasted through from beginning to end. It was a book to dip into randomly, trusting that it would open to the right page in the right hour.

In a chapter titled, "The Animal Self," Ash read:

> *You can go anywhere.*
> *You can do anything.*
> *You can be anyone.*
> *This chapter will show you how.*

Ash closed the heavy tome. He looked up—a solitary crow swooped low and perched on a nearby garden post. It cawed, a throaty chuckle, as if trying to speak. Its goth feathers shone under the high, blistering sun. "I want to fly like you," Ash murmured.

Mr. Do glanced up at Ash from under his wide-rimmed straw hat. He had been pruning back some dead summer flowers—a practice called "deadheading," Ash later learned. The gardener asked, "So you like my garden?"

Startled from his dreaming, Ash answered, "Oh, yes. It's peaceful here."

"A lot of work. But good work." Mr. Do then spoke a phrase in his native Korean, followed by the English translation: "At the end of hardship comes happiness."

Ash was surprised to hear himself volunteer to help. Did those words actually leave his lips? Maybe it was Willow's influence—or her absence. She'd been busy all day with work. Perhaps he missed her.

Mr. Do squeezed a water bottle and sprayed a mist over the plants. "Summer gets very hot. Plants suffer. You can help me water."

"Now?"

"Never during the high sun. Early morning or late in the day. Much better."

"Is that all the help you need?" Ash asked.

Mr. Do waved a hand. "Much to do, always. A healthy garden starts with healthy soil. Must keep the soil moist. I use fertilizer and cover the soil with cedar mulch to retain moisture. It helps prevent weeds, too."

And so they chatted amiably for the first time—Ash and the old Korean man—about pruning and weeding and pesky aphids. "You like the book?" Mr. Do asked, indicating *The Book of Liminal Spaces* on the boy's lap.

Ash covered it protectively with both hands, obscuring the cover. He offered no reply.

Willow bellowed something from across the parking lot.

Ash turned, irritated. He pantomimed with a hand cupped around his ear, the other hand palm up. *I can't hear you.* It seemed wrong to be screaming back and forth while sitting in Mr. Do's Magic Garden.

Willow approached. "Have either of you seen Kristoff? I can't find him anywhere."

"Nope," Ash replied.

They both looked to Mr. Do. The man snipped off the end of a dead flower with a small pair of scissors. He touched the plant's leaves, checking their undersides. Satisfied, he peeled off his gardening gloves. He would not be rushed.

"I checked everywhere, twice," Willow informed them. "He's just . . . gone."

"The laundry room?" Mr. Do asked.

"No."

"The office?"

"Locked," Willow replied.

Mr. Do pondered that for a moment. At last, he said, "It is not like Kristoff to disappear like that. I will go see."

He closed the rabbit gate behind him.

Willow plopped down on the ground beside Daisy, stroking her warm fur. The dog stretched out, basking in her affection. "How's the book?" asked Willow.

"It's good. A little confusing. Half the time I'm not sure what it's talking about," Ash confessed. "And the other half I'm just totally lost!"

They both laughed.

Willow sat up, leaning on an arm. She asked, "You haven't been sending me creepy texts, have you?"

"What?"

"I've gotten some strange texts today. Were they from you?"

"I don't even know what you're talking about," Ash said.

"If you lie to me, Ash, I'll know," Willow warned her brother. "You are the world's worst liar."

"Well?" Ash asked. "What does your lie detector tell you? Do you believe me or not?"

Willow's eyes narrowed in concentration. "You're not lying."

Ash nodded, satisfied.

"You don't know anyone with the initials A.F., do you?"

"Why are you asking?"

"Beats me," Willow said. "Oh! I forgot to tell you—I got creepy vibes from that guy in room six."

"The bald dude?"

"With the mirror shades, yeah." Willow told him about their encounter. And the elaborate computer setup in his room. "I asked Kristoff at lunch how long he was staying. Kristoff said it was open-ended."

"What's that mean?"

"He told Kristoff that—and I quote—he would stay 'for as long as it takes.'"

Nobody liked the sound of that.

Not even the crow still perched on the fence, eavesdropping.

ELEVEN

THE UFO "WACKY WEIRDOS"—as Willow affectionately called them—took over the picnic area for dinner and stayed late into the night. "To be fair," Willow said to the family seated at their customary picnic table, "they seem nice enough. Besides, I like it when people get geeked out about stuff, no matter what it is— Dungeons and Dragons, comic books, Marvel movies, bizarre German prog rock, UFOs, Irish clog dancing—whatever."

"We might need a UFO to take us away from here," Mr. McGinn grumbled.

"Really, Dad?" Ash asked. "Would you *really*

want to be abducted by aliens?"

Mr. McGinn didn't answer. He just frowned at his shoes.

"Greetings, Earthlings," Willow said in a high-pitched robotic voice. "Take me to your pizza."

"What?" Ash snorted, turning to Willow. "That's your impression of an alien?"

"I'm speculating, Ash. I don't know!" Willow protested.

"Personally, I admire their enthusiasm," Mrs. McGinn said, returning to the original subject. "They seem like a fun group of young people. I agree with Willow. It's soooo much better than people who are bored by everything. Nothing's more boring than a person who thinks everything is boring! That's why I love your father. He has more enthusiasm than a bus full of little kids going to the zoo."

Mr. McGinn gave his wife a wan smile. He hadn't felt enthusiastic in days. "I try," he said softly.

"I know you do," she answered.

Ugh, tender moments, Willow thought. She watched with interest as the UFO crowd, presumably after a long day at the convention downtown, dragged chairs over to an unused firepit. Several of them went out to scrounge for deadfall at the edge of the forest—and soon they built a roaring fire. Orange, red, and yellow tongues licked the sky.

"That gives me an idea," Mrs. McGinn said. "I'll be right back."

"Where to, darling?" Mr. McGinn asked.

She placed a finger across her lips and headed to the car.

After days of explorations, the McGinns had learned that they could travel into town—it wasn't much, just a few traffic lights on Main Street—but no farther. It was as if they lived inside a bubble. Ten minutes later, Mrs. McGinn plopped a reusable shopping bag in Willow's lap. It contained marshmallows, chocolate bars, and a box of graham crackers.

"S'mores!" the kids exclaimed.

"You can share them with those folks by the fire," Mrs. McGinn said.

"Aren't you coming?" Ash asked.

"No, your father and I are happy here," their mother answered. She reached out for her husband's hand. "We'll sit here for a while, make sure everything's okay. Besides, you are probably tired of spending so much time with your fuddy-duddy parents."

Willow didn't argue with that.

On cue, a roar of laughter—hoots and clapping—erupted from the firepit.

The cheers grew even louder when Willow and Ash arrived, offering to share s'mores with everyone.

"There is a god!" one of them exclaimed.

Seven people were seated around the fire—with only one open seat. But the big guy in a Hawaiian shirt, Todd, quickly offered his seat to Willow.

"Oh, you don't have to—"

"No biggie," he told Willow. "I'll just grab another lounge chair from the pool area."

At first, Ash felt extremely awkward. Super aware of the age gap. It felt like everyone was staring at him. But after a few minutes, he realized that no one seemed all that interested.

True fact: *S'mores make everything better.*

After a search for long sticks and much debate about proper marshmallow-roasting techniques, Willow and Ash had learned everyone's names: Todd, Joris (in black slacks), Ren (supercute in rainbow-dyed hair),

Monica, (the woman who had been at the office counter the other day), a quiet guy named Darwin (still in flannel pajama bottoms), an extremely hairy guy that everyone called "Sash" for Sasquatch, and last but not least, Velma. Velma was dressed in an orange long-sleeve top, a red skirt, and orange socks pulled up to her knees. She had a pixie haircut and large, square glasses.

Ash said, "Wow, Velma, you look like—"

"Velma from Scooby Doo!" several voices chirped, followed by laughter.

"Jinkies, I get that a lot," Velma said, pushing the glasses farther up the bridge of her nose.

"There's a contest," Joris explained. "Velma is dressed for success."

"What can I say, I'm in it to win it," Velma said.

More laughter all around.

"Ruh-roh!" Todd exclaimed when his marshmallow burst into flames. He swallowed it anyway.

Zoinks!

Ash spied his mother walking up to the group. The tips of his ears turned red with embarrassment. Everyone on the planet had a birth mother, of course, but

58

the last thing Ash wanted was for these people to meet *his* mother. Oh, the horror, the horror.

Todd gallantly stood and offered up his lounge chair.

"Oh, no, thanks," Mrs. McGinn demurred. She smiled at the group. "I hope my children aren't invading your space—"

"Everyone's welcome," Monica said. "Besides, I have three younger siblings. Compared to them, your kids are great!"

Other voices echoed in agreement.

"And the s'mores are perfection," Sash said gratefully.

Mrs. McGinn turned to Willow and Ash. "Okay then. Don't be up too late, kids. Your father and I will be heading in soon."

And that was that. Ash looked at the faces around the fire. No one seemed to care. The sky didn't fall. His mother came and left, and everything was perfectly fine.

"She's not so bad, you know," Willow whispered as if reading his thoughts.

"I propose a toast," Joris announced, rising to his

feet. "Two toasts, actually. First, to our new friends—the tree people—Willow and Ash! You came offering gifts, and we ate them gladly."

The tree people. Ash liked that.

Todd burped sarcastically.

Joris pretended to be annoyed. "As I was saying before I was so rudely interrupted," he continued. "I'm glad you all came to the UFO Fest. Here's to you, my friends. To the dreamers. The believers. The crazy ones. The misfits, the rebels, the troublemakers. You are the ones who see things differently. Who imagine distant worlds in the night sky. Visitors from far-off galaxies. You are beautiful geniuses, each one of you. And to quote my dear old mama, 'Ya'll know how to have a good time, too!' Together, we can change the world. Cheers, my friends!"

Joris got a big round of applause for that—along with a warm hug from Ren. When Ash looked back, he noticed his parents heading to their room, holding hands. His father said something and his mother laughed. It was nice to see. Just a glimpse. A picture. Maybe everything was going to be all right after all.

TWELVE

REN AND JORIS found a working outlet by the pool. In no time, they grabbed an extension cord and put up holiday lights around the pavilion. Sash played music on a Bluetooth speaker. Working on her fourth s'more, Willow asked, "So do you guys really believe in this UFO stuff?"

The circle grew quiet.

Ash glanced at his sister, worried that she had said exactly the wrong thing. This was fun, hanging out with older people. He didn't want Willow to ruin everything.

Todd poked his stick into the fire. Bright embers

floated to the sky, riding currents of hot air. He finally said, "I would turn that question around. How in the world do people *not* believe in UFOs?"

"Oh, boy, here it comes," Monica joked.

Todd jabbed the stick again. More sparks flew. "I'll keep it simple. We all know that our solar system has eight planets. We'll leave Pluto's feelings aside for the moment. It is estimated that there are one hundred billion planets in the Milky Way galaxy, which is where our solar system is located. *One hundred billion.* That's the number one followed by eleven zeros. A scientific study published in the *Astronomical Journal*—I have the latest issue in my van, if you want to read it—estimates that three hundred million of those planets have the right ingredients for life. Size, temperature, atmosphere, etcetera.

"In 2021, NASA's New Horizons space probe was used to estimate that the universe contains roughly two hundred billion galaxies." Todd paused, never taking his eyes off Willow. "Personally, I think that number is low. But I ask you, given those figures, how can there *not* be life on other planets? We humans are so small, yet we think we're so great. In the grand scope of things, we're just specks of dust. How can anyone possibly believe that we are the only ones flying around in space?"

Willow nodded, trying to absorb all the stray facts. Mathematics wasn't exactly her happy place. One thing was clear: *These folks took this stuff very seriously.*

Lightening the mood, Ren added, "However, I still maintain that Todd burps louder than any creature in our solar system."

Todd thundered a gastric reply: *BWURP!*

That broke the tension.

Joris said, "People have been reporting eyewitness accounts of unidentified flying objects for decades. Pilots, ordinary citizens, military personnel. But when people try to tell others about it, they get laughed at, ridiculed."

"The black swan theory," Darwin mumbled.

"Exactly," Velma said, looking from Ash to Willow. "Most people think all swans are white. No one believes in rare black swans—until they see one."

"People won't change their minds unless"—Todd pointed an index finger skyward—"aliens come along and take them up, up, and away. Then they start believing real fast."

"Nonbelievers become believers." Ren snapped her fingers. "Boom."

Ash wondered what they knew about liminal spaces. Probably a lot. "You guys are, like, amazing. I mean it. You make being smart seem cool. Forget aliens. I didn't even know there *were* black swans!"

"You two are pretty awesome yourselves," Ren said. "If anyone is going to save our planet—it'll be young people like you."

"I heard a joke today," Velma announced. "Why don't aliens eat clowns?"

She waited a beat and said, "They taste funny."

Groans all around. Except for one ripple of laughter: *Hee-hee, hee-haw, hee-hee.* Ash's ears pricked up. He knew that laugh. He'd heard it before. He looked at Darwin, the quiet one. Mr. Pajama Bottoms. This was the guy who watched him return to his room late at night. What did he say?

What you been up to, bro?

It might have been nothing. Just a teasing laugh at the end of a long, long night. *Hee-hee, hee-haw, hee-hee.*

Ash decided that he'd keep a close eye on the one named Darwin.

Willow's phone pinged. She glanced at it:

A.F.: Your friend is in danger.

Willow typed a quick response.

Willow: My brother, Ash?
A.F.: No, your friend. Grave danger.
Willow: Who is this???

"Why is the UFO Fest held in this town?" Ash asked. "I mean, out of all the places."

Todd replied, "There are festivals all around the country. Roswell, New Mexico, most famously. Vegas has a killer one. But why specifically here? Legend has it that years ago a UFO landed right near this spot. Supposedly somewhere back in those woods behind the motel."

"You're kidding."

"That's the story, yeah."

"And do you believe it?" Ash asked.

Monica snickered. "Todd believes everything. There isn't a conspiracy theory he doesn't believe."

Todd grinned. "Look, there were witnesses. People talked about it. They wrote about it in their diaries. Do I believe it? Sure, I do. I'd bet my last marshmallow on it. The only problem I have is the landing spot. Why would a spaceship land in the middle of a forest? Why not pick a clearing? Extraterrestrials wouldn't just drop down on a bunch of trees."

Willow glanced at Ash. He was thinking the same thing. The scary place where they found Daisy, tangled in vines. It felt haunted. Unreal. Not of this world.

"I think we've been there," Ash said. "A perfectly round, flat clearing where nothing grows. It's back in those woods. Not too far."

Willow felt goose bumps along her skin. Just thinking about it—the rush of memories—made her skin crawl.

Joris leaned forward. In a hushed voice, he asked, "Can you take us there tomorrow?"

THIRTEEN

THE WOLF OUTSIDE Exit 13 Motel was howling, howling, howling.

It sounded like a storm brewing. Wind bending trees, tree limbs cracking. But when Willow listened closely, there was no wind. The only sound was the ghostly howls of the dire wolf. No other wolf answered; it was alone and, perhaps, *upset*. Was that even possible? Unlike Ash, Willow hadn't actually *seen* the wolf in real life yet—but she had heard its howls.

Daisy restlessly circled the blanket on the floor. Pulled at it with her teeth, tugged, poked at it, and got it tangled up in her paws. The goldendoodle finally plopped down. She whined. Willow reached down and placed a hand on Daisy's rump.

"I've never heard the wolf like this before, LB," Willow said to the darkness.

"Same," Ash replied from his bed.

And she was right. Tonight, the wolf sounded troubled, pained. It began in a mournful, high-pitched moan—like a whale song. Eerie and sorrowful. And slowly built into a deeper, full-throated howl. *Owoooooo.* A cry for help.

Ash knew what the wolf wanted.

Or *who* it wanted.

You'll have to wait until tomorrow, he told the wolf in his thoughts. *You can tell me your troubles tomorrow.*

But to Willow he said, "Wolves are territorial. It might just be saying, 'I am here, this place is mine.'" He didn't believe his own words. He just wanted his sister to relax. It was after midnight and they both needed to sleep. It had been a late night. And tomorrow . . .

"I don't think so," Willow replied. She tossed in bed, flipping over the pillow. "It's trying to communicate something. What do you think it's saying, Ash? You know things."

"It's saying, 'Go to sleep, Willow,'" Ash replied.

Easier said than done. Willow felt wide-awake, puzzling over the mysterious texts. Could they be correct? Was Kristoff—what was the phrase?—in *grave danger*? As in deadly? Kristoff had disappeared after lunch and still hadn't returned. Fortunately Mr. Do stepped up to take the front desk. He said these things happened from time to time. That it was no concern. But Willow could see the creases in his forehead. The way his lips downturned into a frown. The motel caretaker was worried, too. This wasn't normal.

Did it all connect?

The howling wolf, the worry, and Kristoff?

Was there a thread that ran through all three?

Her churning mind returned to the texts. Who was sending them? Willow tried process of elimination. It had to be someone from the motel. No one else, none of her friends from home, could reach her. Ash denied it. She believed him. That left her parents, Kristoff, and Mr. Do. What about the man from room 6? A very creepy thought. She would have to learn more about that dude. A little spying when he left the room. But Willow had a strong feeling that the mysterious

messenger was an ally of some kind. Not a friend-
friend, not someone she knew, but on her side. The
UFO crowd? No, she had received a text when they
were sitting around together. Unless she missed something, it couldn't be them. Her thoughts returned
again to the man in room 6. He didn't seem like an
ally at all.

On impulse, she tapped out a message on her
phone:

Willow: Do you believe in UFOs?

The answer was immediate:

A.F.: Of course!
Willow: Ha!
Willow: I am worried about Kristoff.

She waited several minutes for an answer.

A.F.: We all are.

FOURTEEN

THE LAST TIME Ash had ventured into the forest, it had been night. He had walked trancelike, shivering in a slantways rain. Trees damp and dripping. The ancient forest whispering his name. Shadow upon shadow. He felt chilled at the memory. The terror of that night. How in the darkness he had come to the clearing and crossed over, into the beyond. How he had returned clutching a water-drenched, half-dead cat.

This time, he told himself, would be different.

This time, he would *not* travel beyond the clearing.

It was daylight. And he was not alone.

How bad could it be?

Ash and Daisy paused at a spot where the towering pines assembled. Sunlight streaked though the branches, dappled on the fallen pine needles. The group behind him chattered noisily, stomping like cattle. Todd, Joris, Ren, Sash, and Darwin. Monica and Velma had opted out, intending to eat at a vegan place in town. "I don't hike, period," Monica admitted last night. "Not my jam."

Willow had work back at the motel.

The group gathered for a water break. "You're a sweet, sweet dog," Ren told Daisy. "I have a bullmastiff at home. One hundred and twenty-five pounds of muscle. Named Mulder after, you know, the character in the *X-Files*. Man, I crushed hard on that guy when I was a kid." She scratched behind Daisy's ears.

"Okay, that's it! I've already been bitten by, like, twelve thousand blood-sucking mosquitoes," Todd complained. He looked flushed and sweaty. They'd only been walking for twenty minutes. "I keep killing 'em and they keep coming. It's like the Battle of Helm's Deep from *The Lord of the Rings*."

"Right, sure, Todd. Slapping at bugs," Joris teased.

"That's exactly the same thing as Aragorn and Legolas fighting off an army of Saruman's Orcs."

"Here." Darwin unzipped his pack and handed over a can of bug spray. "Lay it on thick, bro."

Ash looked around. Today, the forest was silent. The trees were not talking to him. Probably because he was not alone. The path was clear. He felt safe and secure. "Ready?"

"Let's do this," Joris said, patting him on the back.

They kept walking.

The trail grew narrower. The underbrush crowded in. Vines choked trees, writhed on the forest floor like snakes. "Watch your step," Ash warned. "Don't leave the trail."

The trees huddled closer, blocking out the lowering sun.

The forest gradually darkened to a semi-twilight.

The joking and laughter grew quiet. The hikers fell into a steady rhythm. One foot in front of the other. Daisy stayed in the lead. Sometimes she'd scamper ahead but would always pause to wait or backtrack, nosing up against Ash before again racing to the front.

The group straggled. Ash and Joris in front. Sash

and his enormous, scruffy beard were next. (Sash reminded Ash of Yukon Cornelius from *Rudolph the Red-Nosed Reindoor*. "Bumbles bounce!") Ren was doing her own thing, pausing to marvel at exotic mushrooms, enjoying nature. Ren was fit and athletic, so keeping up was not a problem for her. Darwin and Todd toiled in the rear.

"Hey, Joris," Ash asked. "Do you know about liminal spaces?"

"Whoa. How old are you, kid?"

"Almost twelve."

"And you are interested in liminal spaces? I'm impressed."

Ash shrugged. "I'm not even sure what it means."

Joris pulled off his glasses, wiping them on his T-shirt. He held them up to the light. Replaced them on his nose. "Okay, let's see. Liminal spaces. It's like . . . the places in-between. Imagine someone who lives in an airport, living in a space *between* destinations. Not quite anywhere. Does that make sense?"

Ash concentrated, faltered.

Joris tried again, "Are you familiar with the concept of limbo?"

Before Ash could answer, Sash began singing, "Sitting here in limbo . . ."

Ren joined in, "Like a bird without a song . . ."

They'd been listening to Ash's conversation.

Joris smiled, grooving to the song. "Liminal spaces are betwixt and between, neither this nor that, a phase between the world you know . . . and the unknown."

Ash wondered if Exit 13 Motel was a liminal space. Could that be it? Had his family been caught in an in-between space?

Neither, nor.

Like a doctor's waiting room.

Betwixt and between.

He smiled at Joris. "Yeah, that helps, thanks."

"Think about a butterfly *before* it becomes a butterfly," Joris said. "The transition from egg, to larva, to chrysalis, and finally to butterfly! Those are liminal phases."

"How much farther?" Todd called out. "My dogs are barking."

"What?" Ash turned to Joris.

"It means his feet are hurting," Joris explained.

"Typical Todd. He only complains when his lips are moving."

"Not far. Just up this hill," Ash called back.

"A hill? You're killing me, kid! I thought this was supposed to be fun," Todd grumbled.

Ash suddenly stopped, seized by a sharp pain in his head. He leaned up against the bole of an oak.

Two voices reached his skull.

One said, "You okay, kid? Here, take a break, drink some water."

The other voice came from *inside* his skull. It called out weakly, *Help them, Ash. Come find them before it's too late.*

Ash gulped down the water. He blinked to clear his head. Through the trees, dim in the gathering fog, he saw the shape of the wolf. Bushy tail, sharp ears, fearsome snout.

Red eyes watching him.

FIFTEEN

IT WAS 4:00 in the afternoon and Kristoff still hadn't returned. Something was wrong.

Mr. Do filled in, performing Kristoff's duties. Willow handled the housekeeping. Every hour or so, she entered the office. "Any news?"

Mr. Do shook his head. Not a word.

Willow lingered in the lobby. "How long have you worked here, Mr. Do?"

"Long time," he answered without taking his eyes off the computer screen.

"Does Kristoff's mother need anything? I could help with food or—"

"All taken care of," the handyman replied. And added after a pause, "You are kind to ask."

"I was wondering . . ."

He looked up. "Yes?"

"The guest in room six."

"Mr. Hoover."

"What's the deal with that guy? He was super unfriendly yesterday. Something about him feels off. When everyone was at the festival yesterday, he stayed at the motel. He said not to disturb him. But should I still, like, clean the room or—"

"If the DO NOT DISTURB sign is hanging from the doorknob, you do not disturb," Mr. Do replied matter-of-factly.

"Not even for garbage or towels?"

"Do not disturb."

"Oh." Willow paused, shifting strategies. "So do you think he's here for the UFO thing?"

Mr. Do looked at Willow, not unkindly. "First job, no?"

She nodded.

"It is not our job to ask questions." He rhythmically slapped an open palm with the back of his hand.

"Some guests want, want, want. They keep us running. Other guests—they want to be left alone. Easier that way."

Willow sat in one of the office's three mismatched chairs. "Are you trapped here, too, Mr. Do? Like us?"

Mr. Do's lips tightened. He returned his gaze to the computer. "The motel is different for every guest. They come and they go. Some stay longer than others."

It was frustrating. Mr. Do had a way of answering questions without answering them. He talked in riddles. Willow wondered if it was a cultural thing? Or just the way he was? A keeper of secrets? "Do you worry that something happened to him? Kristoff, I mean." Something about saying Kristoff's name out loud brought her emotions to the surface. A crack in her voice. "Like, I don't know, something bad?"

"You think he was abducted by UFO?" Mr. Do grinned, pleased with his joke. Willow didn't laugh. He saw the wet shimmer in her eyes. He had heard, and ignored, the fear in her voice. "I am sorry. But worry does not help bring the water to a boil. Is the laundry finished? The walkway swept? Every room spotless? Work will help your heart and mind."

Movement outside the window caught his attention. His jaw clenched and eyes narrowed. Willow followed Mr. Do's gaze. Mr. Hoover from room 6 strode purposefully to his car. He pulled out of the parking lot, driving fast.

Willow felt it in her bones. A gut instinct. This guy had something to do with Kristoff's disappearance. After all, the anonymous message had already been sent: *Beware of the man in room six.* Willow made a decision. "You are right, Mr. Do. I have to hand it to you. When you know, you know! I'll go check the laundry and, um, I still have a few . . . other things . . . to do."

The old man nodded distractedly.

He was playing Tetris on the computer.

A few moments later, Willow opened the door to room 6. She pulled the curtains closed, not wanting to be seen by anyone passing by. Willow scanned the room. The computers hummed softly. The screens were blank, in rest mode.

The previous day, over Mr. Hoover's shoulder, she saw folders and papers. What a name, huh? *Hoover.* Like the vacuum cleaner. *He sucks.* Willow chuckled to herself. She popped her earbuds in out of habit; music helped her think. Where were those folders now? She began to search the room.

Under the bed, in the bathroom, in the closet. An aluminum suitcase had the name X-STAR CORP stamped on it. She'd have to look that up later. On the night table, beside the phone, sat a wooden carving. It was a—well, it was hard to tell exactly what it was. A sick duck? A mangled bear? Hoover was no Michelangelo, that much was for sure. Willow kept moving, searching quickly, unsure of what she was seeking. Some evidence of Kristoff? Mr. Hoover was a precise person, everything in its place. Two pairs of shoes in a tidy row. One solitary wrapper in the garbage can. An Almond Joy candy bar. Shredded coconut. How could anyone eat that stuff? Gross, puke.

Willow looked through the clothes drawers. In the bottom drawer, beneath the socks, she found a large knife in a sheath. Okay, that was sort of normal. All sorts of folks had knives for plenty of reasons other than stabbing people. But still, Willow's heart climbed into her throat. She audibly gasped and shut the drawer. She felt stressed and anxious. Willow wanted to get out of there, *fast*. But at the time, here was her best chance to solve the mystery. Kristoff was missing. He was in *grave danger*. Nerves vibrating, Willow forced herself to be brave. She sat before the main computer, hit a key, and the machine leaped to life. It was password protected. Probably encrypted. *Figures*, she thought. She'd seen detectives solve passwords with guesses. It was worth a try. Willow began to type: H–O–O–V–E–R–6 . . .

She did not hear the door slowly, cautiously open.

(The closed curtains had alerted him.)

When Willow finally turned her head, there he stood, glaring. Dressed in the same black suit. Bald, shiny head. Mirror sunglasses. For the first time, there was a smile on Mr. Hoover's face.

He actually looked happy to see her.

Not good.

SIXTEEN

WHEN THEY FIRST REACHED the clearing, no one could believe it. Which was curious, because, after all, this was *a group of believers.* UFOs, alien abductions, wild conspiracies. *Believing* was how they rolled. Sash literally wore a denim jacket with the word BELIEVE painted on the back in capital letters.

They stood in the perfect circle of a flat hilltop—five UFO fanatics and eleven-year-old Ash McGinn.

Where nothing—absolutely nothing—grew.

Not a flower, not a weed. Not a bird or bug. Not a single living thing.

It almost felt wrong to stand there. As if the site

itself was hostile to life. A place they shouldn't be.

"Unearthly," Ren whispered.

"Alien," Sash murmured.

"What do you think, Joris?" Todd held out his arms. "Sixty, seventy-five feet in diameter?"

"Sounds right."

Ash stood off to the side. The voice in his head had subsided. But he felt suddenly drained, weakened. He knew that the wolf was near. Soon, he hoped, it would be time to go back. Leave this place. Return to the security of the motel. Now that they'd seen it, they should go. Daisy protectively stayed close, which was sweet but not very reassuring. A goldendoodle would be worthless in a fight. Ash noticed that the weather on top of the hill was different. Colder, damper. The fog was growing thicker, rubbing against his ankles like a starving cat.

"What happened here?" Sash asked. He bent to scratch at the dry, lifeless soil. "Look around. We are surrounded by old-growth forest for miles and miles. How do you explain something like this?"

"Landing site," Joris said.

"That's just one hypothesis," Ren remarked, unconvinced.

"I'm getting shivers right now," Todd confessed. "I believe that aliens once stood here in this very spot."

"How is this not a thing?" Darwin asked. "Everyone should know about this place. Scientists should be studying it."

"Maybe they have," Joris suggested.

"Government cover-up," Todd said. "Happens all the time."

"But why would they hide it?" Darwin asked the group.

Todd shook his head dismissively. "If normal people had any idea, Darwin, they'd freak out. Why go to work tomorrow if alien spaceships are zooming around in our backyard? So the government keeps the lid on it."

By now, Ash has learned that once Todd got going, nothing was going to stop him. Todd's voice grew louder and more excited. "The government has been in contact with alien species for decades, at least since the 1950s. Fossilized microbes were discovered in meteorite ALH 84001 in Antarctica! The SETI project has received signals on three occasions—from the same region of space! I bet they even have trade agreements! We swap technology! Microchips! Where do you think we got that technology? Alien tech! Ancient space travelers! That explains the pyramids! The Moai stone heads on Easter Island! We're just a new market for them. Aliens got us hooked on cell phones!"

"I don't know about all that," Ren said doubtfully.

"The government can't hide this stuff forever," Sash said. "The truth is out there."

Joris said, "Let's face it. The discovery of alien species would be the biggest scientific discovery in the history of the human race. It will blow minds. Some Fourth of July, we're going to look up and there will be a giant spaceship hovering over the White House!"

"I think I've seen that movie, bro," Darwin said.

After a while, Ash stopped listening. These guys had some pretty wild ideas. He wondered if they really believed them. Maybe it was just for fun. Smart folks playing with ideas. Ash's feet took him to the far side of the clearing. Daisy nipped nervously at his pants leg and whined. Ash didn't slow down. He was like a fish caught on a hook. Something in the far woods, something beyond, was reeling him in.

That's where the wolf now sat. Patiently waiting.

As Ash drew near, the wolf walked deeper into the woods. Down into a dark ravine. The wolf paused and looked back. As if to say, *Are you coming?* Ash hesitated. The wolf took another two steps. Stopped. And again looked back over its muscular haunches. Red eyes beseeching. Almost pleading.

Please, hurry up. Be brave. Rescue them. Rescue all of them.

Without looking back, without telling the others, Ash followed.

For the second time in his life, Ash left the clearing and crossed over. The wolf walked down into a tangled growth of twisting, wind-ravaged oaks. A little-used path into another world.

A few minutes later, Ren looked around. The fog had rolled in thick. It was up to the top of her socks. Strange for a summer evening. "Hey, you guys? Anybody seen Ash?"

SEVENTEEN

WILLOW INSTANTLY STOOD UP. She sputtered out an explanation. "I was in here—for the dirty towels!—and I saw your computer and—the Wi-Fi around here—just totally blows and like—I'm such a computer geek and—I didn't mean to—"

"Sit," Mr. Hoover said.

Willow sat. "I'm really sorry. I know it was wrong. I can see—"

"You need to be quiet right now," he demanded.

Willow decided to be quiet. See how this played out. She was dealing with a displeased doofus.

He glanced around the room, checking to see if

anything had been disturbed. He adjusted the carving—Willow still hadn't decided if it was a bad attempt at a goose, or maybe a frog? No matter what, it was the worst wood carving in the History of Wood Carvings. Yet Hoover seemed proud of it. He turned it so that the goose-frog-creature thingy aligned perfectly with the edge of the table. Lifting the mattress, he pulled out some folders. "Still sealed," he murmured. In bold black letters, one file was labeled EXIT 13. Another read KRISTOFF. Willow couldn't make out the others.

(She never thought to look under the mattress. Rookie mistake.)

Muttering to himself, the man paced the room. "Think, Hoover, think. What to do, what to do?"

(Yeah, that's right. He called himself Hoover. Total loon!)

Willow slowly stood, trying to remain calm, cool, and collected. "I think I should go now."

"You should have *thought* before breaking into my room," Hoover said. "Touching my personal items. *Sit down!*" He ran his hand over the top of his head the way bald people often did on television shows. They must like the way it feels. Smooth as a cue ball.

89

Willow wondered if she'd ever have the guts to shave her own head—just for that snazzy cue-ball feeling. No, she decided, probably not.

"Please, Mr. Hoover, sir. I'm totally sorry. I was wrong. It will never happen again."

He held up a hand to silence her apology. He brought the crook of an index finger to his pursed lips. "You have a master key, correct?"

Willow nodded.

"And you can get into any room?"

"I'm not sure—no!—not any—"

"Don't lie to me!" His petulant voice rose to nearly a squeal. "You are not allowed to lie. We need to reach an agreement. That's all. A mutual understanding between two parties. No one gets hurt."

That's when Willow felt it for the first time. A wave of fear. He might be a Major Dork, but this Hoover dude could be dangerous. *Who mentioned anything about getting hurt?* She was trapped in a room with an FBI-type guy who she could not trust. He may have had a ten-cent brain, but still: He was trouble. "Mr. Do will come looking for me," Willow said, not quite believing it.

A crow cawed outside the window. Insistent. Again

and again. Hoover did not seem to notice. "We are going to walk together to a room that is two doors down. It is a room without a number. You will use your key. And we will step inside together."

"But—"

"Understood?" he said. "That's our bargain. You help me, and I won't tell on you."

Willow nodded. The phone vibrated in her back pocket. She wrapped her arms around her chest. Some instinct told her not to answer the phone in front of him.

"Let's go," Hoover said.

In a minute, they were inside the Unnumbered Room. The man looked around in triumph. "So this is it." He pointed to the chair in the corner by the lamp. "Sit there and don't move a muscle."

"Like, stay completely totally frozen? Like a Popsicle? Or can I move a teeny-little bit?"

Hoover glared at her.

Willow couldn't help herself. She enjoyed teasing him. But she played along, sitting perfectly motionless. There was an open book on the small table. The pages flickered, as if turned by an invisible hand.

The new page read, "How to Survive Bear Attacks."

Hmmm, curious.

Hoover walked to the bookshelf, fascinated. He ran his fingers across the spines. Willow half turned and slipped the phone from her pocket. There was a text. It read, simply:

> **A.F.: Ask to go to the bathroom.**

Willow tucked the phone away. "I have to—may I—go to the bathroom—please—sir?"

Hoover frowned. "Really?"

"I'm sorry. I have to go." Willow squirmed in her seat.

"Hold it," he said.

"Not an option, seriously," Willow said. "I have a thing with my bladder. It's like the size of a chipmunk's. When I gotta go, it's like, I don't know, completely bananas. Whatever muscle people have that keeps pee inside them, I don't have it. The pee just gushes out. It's gross, and I'm sorry, but that's my life."

Hoover frowned. Keeping an eye on his captive, he backpedaled to the bathroom door. Peeked inside.

Toilet, sink, shower. The lone window was narrow and locked. She couldn't possibly climb through to escape without breaking glass. He'd be listening for it. "Two minutes. No tricks."

"Thank you," Willow said.

The moment she entered the bathroom, her phone buzzed again:

> **A.F.: You are in the presence of a dangerous man. Pay close attention. There is a can of bear spray under the sink. Hide it somewhere on your body. Mr. Hoover will soon find the hatch. Use the spray first chance you get AFTER he opens the hatch. He will be blinded, but only briefly. There is a flashlight hidden on the wardrobe shelf behind a purple cashmere sweater. You will take the flashlight and climb down the ladder. Move quickly, dear. He will come after you and you must not be caught. Follow the long hallway until you reach the green door. DO NOT open any other doors. Only the green one. No matter**

what. **Be sure to shut the door after you. Good luck.**

"That's long enough!" Hoover called.

Willow wanted to send a quick reply. *Help me. Save me. And where do I hide a can of bear spray on my body? Under my armpit?* Instead, she grabbed the spray and tucked it into the back of her pants. Totally uncomfortable. She flushed the toilet. And Willow, before opening the door, sent out a silent prayer.

Like a kite sailing up to the clouds.

Let's hope this works.

She didn't want to make the Complete and Total Doofus angrier than he already was.

EIGHTEEN

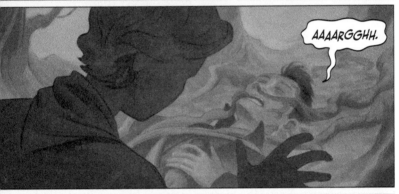

97

NINETEEN

MR. DO HAS SWITCHED to solitaire on the computer. A mindless activity, but it soothes him. The phone rings. He informs the caller, "No vacancy." Not a phrase he recalled ever saying before. *No vacancy.* It sounds harsh, cruel almost. Go away! No vacancy! Is that possible? Through all the years? The motel was never full before? That can't be true. It's that he forgets. They say that sudoku is good for old brains. Keeps the circuits firing. Important to keep the mind sharp. There are herbs and spices in his garden to boost brain health: sage, turmeric, the leaves of the ginkgo to stimulate blood flow to the brain . . .

He likes the girl, Willow. He searches the warehouse of memory for the word. Nothing comes, nothing comes, then—aha!—he retrieves it. *Spunk.* She has spunk, that one. Courageous and determined. Guests come and go and some linger. Mr. Do watches and waits. Hopeful? No, no, that's not the word. Try not to have attachments. No expectations. *What comes, comes.* Hope only gets in the way. He remembers an old life in a different place. Long ago. So much has passed. Surely there is no one there for him anymore. A garden gone fallow. No life to return to.

He keeps turning over cards, arranging columns, losing in solitaire.

He tries not to worry about Kristoff, who has surely gone off and done something dangerous.

An old man trying not to think.

He loses at solitaire again.

It doesn't matter.

A game of chance and luck.

That's life, no? A spoonful of skill and a mountain of circumstance. One plays the cards one has been dealt. With dignity and grace.

Hope, worry, fear, love. Mr. Do pushes those things

away—like clearing clutter off a desk with the sweep of an arm. One must empty oneself. Cleanse the mind and heart—scrub them clean—receive only what is. Not worry about what might be or what once was. The future, the past.

Be here now.

But why this tear falling from his eye?

How the past holds him still. *Lost loves.* Can love ever be, he wonders, truly lost? Like a button popped off a coat? Without thinking, he taps himself in the chest. Three times. Tap, tap, tap. Two children and a wife. He remembers their names.

Sung-Hi, Chelsea, Henry.

Of course, no sign of Kristoff's mother. She is gone, too. Though he heard her complaints in the night. Probably ran off to track the son. He wishes her luck. Such a strange, troubled world.

Why does he feel this melancholy? The girl and her questions. *Stirring dull roots with spring rain.* It is better to forget.

"How long have you worked here, Mr. Do?"

A question without an answer. But he replied, "Long time."

Long time indeed.

Mr. Hoover in room 6. He does not fool Mr. Do. *What comes, comes.*

And so, yes, the boy reads the book.

His power grows.

Perhaps that will be *the way*.

The path to follow.

The journey, finally, home.

He goes to the window. Above, a swirling of crows. They fly and climb, wheel and swoop. He looks for the hawk. Usually, that's all it is. The threat of a hawk is all it takes. Up the crows rise from tree limbs to fill the sky. But there is no danger that he can see.

What do the crows know that he does not?

What danger do they know?

The boy, Ash, promised that he will water the garden this evening. Good for a child to learn about gardens. Caring about life. Tending after it. Sowing and reaping. A time for this . . . a time for that.

The girl works hard, but she is slow. A child still. Everything takes time.

Time, time, time.

There is so much of it.

All that matters, he reminds himself, is the moment. Be here now. Especially in this place. All that time and nothing matters but the one silvery, shimmering instant before us.

A fly lands on the desk. Mr. Do eyes it without turning his head. *Time flies, eh?* The insect crawls around, busy with something, lifts off, circles, lands again. Mr. Do strikes and the fly is caught inside his fist. He brings it to his ear, listens, satisfied.

The old man walks to the door, opens it, extends his arm, and releases the fly outside.

Where is Willow now? Why is she taking so long?

The phone rings. The crows cry. The cards await.

TWENTY

SIT.

HOW TO SURVIVE BEAR ATTACKS

BEAR MACE

creeeaaak

YOU. PULL OPEN THIS HATCH.

DARK DOWN THERE.

BEAR MACE

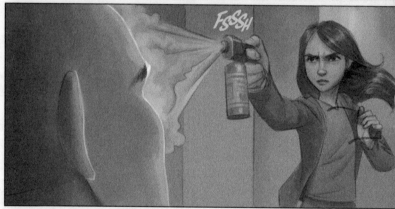

FSSSH

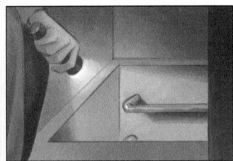

gulp

TWENTY-ONE

ASH GENTLY PLACED the lanky, undernourished puppy to the side on a patch of moss. Its empty belly, swollen from hunger, rose and fell. It was breathing and appeared unharmed. Ash turned his focus back to Kristoff.

Ren was the first to arrive, the rest only steps behind.

For a stunned moment, they all stood clustered together in shock at the scene before them: Ash kneeling beside a limp body on the ground, tangled in plant life. As if it were being reclaimed by the earth. The way a fallen tree trunk is slowly broken down and repossessed by the living earth. Vines and ferns and leafy branches had wrapped themselves around Kristoff. He was entwined, entangled, cocooned, and snarled in undergrowth.

"Whoa," Darwin murmured.

Ren hurried forward and got down to her knees. The others gathered closer. Joris spoke. "Is he alive?"

"I think so, yes," Ash replied.

Kristoff blinked.

"You know him?"

"Yes, Kristoff—from the motel," Ash explained.

Joris said, "We need to get that vine out of his mouth. He'll choke to death."

"How did this happen?" Darwin wondered. He looked around in panic.

"Never mind that," Todd said. "Help me clear away these vines."

Sash produced a pocketknife. It was small but reasonably sharp. He began cutting away at the vines. Kristoff was covered by layers of ferns, wintercreeper, sedum, and knots of ground-crawling vegetation. Ash tore away the leaves and roots that covered Kristoff's face and neck. Stickers ripped his skin, causing him to bleed. Ash sucked on his thumb for an instant, then spit out the blood. Daisy crouched down, motionless, growling in a low, frightened rumble.

Joris grabbed the vine that had snaked into Kristoff's mouth. He tugged gently, slowly, steadily. The vine seemed to resist him. It fought back. "Todd, a little help, please. But don't pull too hard, big guy. Steady and slow."

Sash joined in, too. A life-or-death game of tug-of-war.

Ash kept peeling debris away from Kristoff's face and neck. Kept urging in a fierce whisper, "Hold on, Kristoff, stay with us. We've got you now. We won't let you go."

Slowly, and then in a final burst, they pulled the vine from Kristoff's throat. He coughed, rolled to his side, and wretched a thick stream of black-green bile. Ren rubbed his back, occasionally pounding it to clear his lungs.

Loose vines receded, slithering away like living snakes. Daisy took two leaps after one into the woods—yipped as if she were bitten—and came limping back to safety.

The group paused, panting.

"Help me prop him up," Ash said.

They leaned Kristoff against the base of a tree. Ren gently teased a tendril from out of Kristoff's nose. She brought her index and middle fingers to the side of his neck, over the carotid artery. She stared off, counting the beats. "Pulse is weak. I don't know— it's like he's been poisoned."

It was true. Kristoff's eyes were sunken and red around the edges. His skin was pale and drawn. His face a death mask.

"This place feels toxic," Todd said. "Radiation sickness, maybe."

"Um, guys," Darwin said. "We've got company."

His eyes were wide, scanning the forest floor that surrounded them. It was obscured by thick foliage, ground creepers and masses of ferns, bearberry and juniper, along with a thick mattress of blue-gray fog.

And it was moving.

Writhing. Twisting. Alive.

A hissing sound came to Ash's ears. *Ashes, Ashes, we all fall down.*

"Snakes!" Sash shouted.

111

A vine shot out and wrapped around Darwin's leg. It yanked him to the ground. Darwin fell on his back with a heavy thud, banging his head. He kicked at the vine with his free leg. Another vine joined the fight. And another. Darwin was being dragged into the thick ground cover. Todd grabbed hold of his arms. Joris helped. Ash, too. Sash leaped to Darwin's feet and began sawing away at the vines with his knife.

Ash brushed something from his hair. A leaf or a bug. Out of the corner of his eye, he saw Ren do the same. He looked up. Spiders were dropping down on gossamer threads from the trees, like army paratroopers from a plane. Dozens of them. Hundreds. Ash slapped at his neck. He could feel the microdose of poison from the spider's bite. The bite area already rising to an angry red welt.

He heard Todd roar, "Spiders? Spiders! I hate freaking spiders!"

TWENTY-TWO

WILLOW WAS IN THE DARKNESS, chasing a beam of light. The light bounced with each stride. The ground at her feet was hard, made of solid rock. If she wanted, Willow could reach out her hands to touch the side walls. The ceiling, too, was only a foot over her head. A tall person would have to duck to keep from hitting their head.

Willow had friends who ran cross-country. They were always after her to join up. *It's fun*, they said. *Try it*, they said. Willow never got the appeal. You go to practice . . . and run. The next day . . . run some more. "And guess what, kids?" the track coach would scream. "Today, as an extra bonus, we're all going to run some more!"

Every single day. That's a boatload of running.

In the tunnel, Willow could hear her own steps echoing against the walls. *Clomp, clomp, clomp.* Every once in a while, fifty feet or so, a small round light fixture at ankle level marked the pathway. When she looked ahead, the lights helped her see if the tunnel was curving in a new direction. The footlights outlined the path like lights on an airport runway.

She paused to catch her breath. Willow looked back. A faint flickering light in the distance. Was it the footlights? No, this light was moving like a comet coming this way. Hoover using his phone for light. She heard his heavy steps.

He was gaining on her.

And all this while, not a single door.

What color was she supposed to open?

Willow wasn't sure anymore.

The blue door? The red door?

Willow started running again. She felt a stitch in her side. A jabbing pain.

She ignored it.

Willow thought:

1) Gosh, this is a really long tunnel,
2) Running is evil, and
3) I will never run again for as long as I live.

Willow could understand running *after* something. Like a school bus. Or an escaped pet. A dog that leaped a fence. Or a ball! That made sense. You ran after a ball—could be a soccer ball or a softball—running after a golf ball would be super insane—then you caught up to the ball. The running had a point. A reason to run. But cross-country with Jada and Abby? Forget that. Not happening.

"You won't get away!" Hoover screamed.

Which was impressive, really. To run *and* scream. Just running—that's about all Willow could do at one time. She was glad to have the flashlight in her hand. It was big and heavy. Made of metal. If she bonked someone in the head with it—say, Hoover, for example—it might knock him out. It was good to have a weapon. *Every girl should have one*, Willow thought.

God, running is evil.

Willow transferred the heavy flashlight between her hands and dropped it. The flashlight skittered across the floor. There was the sound of glass breaking. The lens. And the light died with it.

She heard Hoover's footsteps. Steady, strong, and getting closer.

Willow grabbed the phone from her pocket, thumbed it, and turned on the flashlight app. It wasn't nearly as bright. She'd lost valuable time.

"Wait up!" Hoover called. "We can talk about this!"

Talk about this? *Was he bananas*? No, sorry, Hoover. Willow Bliss McGinn was not hanging around for a conversation. Catch ya later!

Willow turned back. She inhaled sharply through her mouth. He was really getting closer now.

Where, oh where, are those dumb doors?

Willow turned on the jets. Nothing motivated a runner like being chased by a lunatic. Or whatever Hoover was. A corporate spy? A government agent? Just an all-around creepy dude with awesome sunglasses? It didn't matter to Willow one way or the other. So long as he didn't catch her.

There, up ahead, a door!

Willow stepped in front of it. The door was blue. Was that the right color? She put her hand on the silver crank handle. One tug downward and she'd be through. Did it really matter which door she opened? Anything to get out of this claustrophobic tunnel.

Willow hesitated, uncertain.

She looked farther down the tunnel. No doors that she could see.

To her right, Hoover, still coming.

She checked the last text from A.F.

> **Follow the long hallway until you reach the green door. DO NOT open any other doors. Only the green one. No matter what. Be sure to shut the door after you. Good luck.**

Long hallway? That was an understatement. She had probably run a mile and a half at an uncomfortable pace. The stitch in her side had gone away. Unfortunately, her lungs felt like they might explode into a million-billion pink, fleshy pieces. Disgusting. Willow took her hand off the door handle.

She kept running.

Hoover was twenty yards away. He looked super angry.

Willow ran a little faster.

Another door!

This one was yellow.

Willow didn't even slow down.

Without glancing back, Willow could sense Hoover gaining ground. The sound of his feet. The sound of his breath. If she hadn't dropped the flashlight—like a total dork!—she could at least enjoy the pleasure of whacking him upside the head with it. But now? There was only one hope.

A green door!

Willow reached for the handle, pulled it down, and pushed through.

She slammed the door shut behind her.

Click. A lock tumbler snapped firmly into place.

She heard Hoover screaming, pounding the door.

Anger management problems, obviously.

The lock held firm.

Willow stood hunched over, hands on her knees, gasping for air. It was all she had left. No energy even to look around.

TWENTY-THREE

SASH LIFTED KRISTOFF across his shoulders. He wrapped his left arm around Kristoff's legs and used that hand to clasp Kristoff's dangling arms. In his free hand, Sash still held the knife. He looked fiercely determined. A mountain man on a mission. "Let's move out!"

"Wait," Ash said. "The puppy. It's gone!"

He stood staring at the mossy area where he had placed the young pup. In all the noise and confusion, did it run away in fear? Alone and helpless in this dark forest?

Joris tugged Ash by the elbow. "There's no time for that. It's not safe here. We gotta go."

Spiders continued to drop down from the trees on silvery threads.

Ash looked around once more, desperately hoping to find the pup. Nowhere. Not here. Gone.

Save them, the voice had said.

Kristoff and the pup.

He had failed.

He helped save one, but not the other.

Save them all.

"Now!" Joris insisted, dragging Ash from the spot.

The gang trudged back up the hill toward the clearing. They slapped at their necks and pulled spiders from their hair. With each step, they seemed to leave the danger farther behind. Sash paused, adjusting Kristoff's body on his shoulders. "You good?" Todd asked.

The bearded man nodded.

Crack. A tree limb above Ash snapped. Ren took two running steps and lunged. She tackled Ash and they tumbled out of the way. The branch crashed to the ground right where he had been standing.

"Ren, my God, if you hadn't—" Darwin said, unable to utter the words. That Ash might have been killed. Felled by a fallen limb.

Ren and Ash lay sprawled on the ground. Too stunned to reply.

Joris looked up, searching the trees.

"No wind," Todd said.

"No," Joris agreed. "What made it break?"

Todd shook his head. He didn't want to even imagine the answer—that the tree *meant* to do it. The slithering vines, the spiders, the trees. All of nature in revolt against them.

They moved farther up the hill. Bedraggled, worn, roasted.

Sash blew air from his mouth and huffed and puffed.

"You sure you've got him?" Joris asked Sash.

Sash nodded. "I volunteer at our local fire department. Small town, no fires, but I did the training."

"Where's the wolf?" Ash asked. "Did it take the puppy?"

He stopped, turned, and looked in every direction.

No one answered. Ren and Joris looked at each other, confused.

"Didn't you see it?" Ash asked the group. "The wolf was pacing back and forth back there. It was with us the whole time."

"Sorry, Ash," Joris said, placing a hand on his shoulder. "We don't see a wolf."

"Well, no, not now—but didn't you? Back there?" Ash asked urgently. "It led me here. I wouldn't have found Kristoff unless the wolf—"

"Easy," Ren said in a soothing voice. "It's okay. First things first. Let's get out of here. Get your friend medical attention."

No one had seen the wolf. Only Ash.

Was it even real?

Was he losing his mind?

Darwin gestured to the right. Daisy was digging a few yards off the trail. "What's Daisy got?"

Ash saw Daisy clawing furiously in the soil. Sprays of dirt flew out of the hole. *What was she up to?* Todd walked over to Daisy. He bent low, peering into the hole. *Hmmmm.* "Sash, take a breather. Darwin, help me here. I need a hand with this." Todd grabbed hold of the end of a heavy chain that Daisy had unearthed. The chain was attached to something still buried in the soil. A thin piece of white metal poked out of the dirt. Darwin grabbed a stick. He started to scrape away at the soil. Todd pulled on the chain, swinging it from side to side to help loosen the prize. Bit by bit, a piece of metal emerged. Slowly the earth released its treasure.

An owl hooted from the trees.

Todd flicked dirt off the object. Brushed and polished it with the side of his forearm sleeve. He held it up above his head for all to see. It was a rectangular warning sign. It read RESTRICTED AREA in large, bold, red letters. Below, in smaller black type: AUTHORIZED PERSONNEL ONLY.

"How long has this been here?" Todd wondered. "Must have been decades, maybe a hundred years."

"I don't understand," Darwin said. "Restricted area? There's nothing here."

"But something *was* here," Ash said with conviction. The others turned to him, surprised by Ash's certainty. "Something old, from another time. Something long buried."

From ten feet beyond the hole came a crackling sound. Like the *zzzzut* of a backyard bug zapper. A bright light forced them to momentarily cover their eyes. The light dimmed to the outline of a rectangle. It was a few feet wide and about six feet in height. And then, suddenly, a door appeared.

An ordinary green door.

A door where no door should ever be.

Here in the middle of nowhere.

The door opened and Willow rushed through. She turned, chest heaving, and slammed the door shut. It closed with an audible click. Willow bent over, fighting to catch her breath. She hadn't seen them yet. Hadn't even looked around.

No one said a word.

It's hard to think of something to say while staring at a miracle.

TWENTY-FOUR

LET'S GET THIS GUY BACK TO THE MOTEL.

WE HAVE A LOT TO TALK ABOUT.

THERE WAS A PUPPY, WILL, THAT KRISTOFF WAS TRYING TO PROTECT.

I THINK WE NEED TO RESCUE IT.

TWENTY-FIVE

WHEN MR. DO realized that Willow would not accept no for an answer, he allowed her into Kristoff's room. "For a short time only. Must rest." But then he added kindly, "A short visit might do him good."

It was a simple bedroom. Neatly arranged. Plants and candles. A yoga mat on the floor. Hand weights. An acoustic guitar on a stand. And books, books, books. The ceiling was painted black, covered in stars. Kristoff lay in bed, propped halfway up with pillows. He looked only slightly better than half dead, which was an improvement over the day before.

And, honestly, "half dead" was not that far away from his normal look.

"Hi," Willow said softly. She pulled a chair closer to the bed. "How are you feeling?"

Kristoff tilted his head this way and that.

"It was scary," she told him. "Seeing you like that. Ash said it was much worse—when he found you."

Kristoff didn't answer. He didn't have the strength. Still seemed zoned out.

"I can see that you are tired," she said. "I won't stay long. I just wanted to give you this." She placed a package of Twizzlers on his bed. "Best medicine in the world."

Kristoff's eyes moved from the candy to Willow. He coughed softly. "Throat," he said hoarsely. He rubbed his throat. "Hurts."

"Shhh, don't talk then," Willow said. "You should have ice cream. I had my tonsils taken out once and they gave me gobs and gobs of ice cream. It was almost worth it."

Kristoff smiled and yawned. His eyes fluttered sleepily.

"What were you doing out there?" Willow asked.

His eyes shuttered closed like a winter window.

Willow sat in silence, watching him sleep. His chest rising and falling with each breath. She felt confused by this troubled boy. Where was his mother? His father? How did he get here, and for how long? She wanted to brush the hair from his face. Heck, she wanted to wash it! Kind of stringy. Maybe Ash was right. Kristoff was too old for her by about two hundred years, give or take a few decades.

Was that even possible? Of course not. And yet . . . at Exit 13, *anything* seemed possible.

Older guys, sigh. This was a little ridiculous. Still cute, though. Even if he could really use a shower. He smelled a little ripe.

◊◊◊

Mr. Do tapped lightly on the door and poked his head inside.

Willow rose and followed him out. They went past a living room area—there was a small kitchen to the right—and to a door that led directly into the office lobby. Willow guessed that's what it was like to run a motel. Your home was your work, your work was your home. It all got mixed up together.

"Are you sure he shouldn't be in the hospital?" Willow asked.

"No hospital," Mr. Do replied.

"But—"

"Kristoff will recover quickly, you'll see."

Willow remembered from before. How he had gotten slashed across the face. But just a few hours later, there was barely a scratch. Chalk up one more mystery to Exit 13 Motel.

Willow wanted to ask about Kristoff's mother. It was weird that she wasn't here. But like the dire wolf, Willow had never actually seen Kristoff's mother. Something told Willow that it wasn't the right time. And besides, Mr. Do wasn't the right person. Not a big talker. Maybe Kristoff would be up for a conversation in a few days. She had so many questions. *Patience, Will*, she told herself. *Wait until he's ready.*

"Mr. Do," Willow said. "I was wondering about, um, the guest in room six."

"Mr. Hoover."

"Yeah."

Mr. Do locked eyes with Willow. For just a moment. But it was long enough. In that fleeting instant, his eyes told her everything.

He knew, he cared, and he understood.

"All gone," Mr. Do said. "We won't see him again."

"What? He checked out?"

"Mm-hmm."

"The stuff in his room?" Willow asked.

"I cleaned up everything. Ready for the next guest."

Willow's eyes went to the window and the parking lot beyond. "His car is still here."

Mr. Do hesitated for a fraction of a second. "Uber, I think. Car trouble. Not my job to ask questions."

"I see," Willow replied. "But—"

"Not your job, either," Mr. Do stated.

"Okay. It's just—you know where we were, don't you?"

The old man rubbed his chin. He made a decision. "Sometimes in life, there are doors. One door, happiness. Another door . . . the wrong path, lost forever."

"He opened the wrong door?" Willow asked.

"So many questions," Mr. Do replied, ushering her out the front door. "Gives Mr. Do a headache. Thank you for coming. Now go. Kristoff will be fine. You'll see."

TWENTY-SIX

ASH READ FROM *The Book of Liminal Spaces.* The heavy book in his hands was awkward and cumbersome. So he lay in bed with a spare pillow on his belly, the hardcover resting on that. His body felt achy and tired. Daisy lay curled up on the floor, perfectly still, still exhausted from yesterday's adventures. The chapter was titled "Transfigurations."

The talented student will eventually be able to feel what another person feels. Not simply to understand, *but to feel it inside one's own self. Another person's loneliness becomes your loneliness. Another person's joy becomes the same joy that you experience. This practice—learning to travel the liminal pathways—can be can also be achieved with animals. Imagine it. Make it happen. Leap with the antelope. Hunt with the mountain lion. Fly with the crow . . .*

Ash felt his forehead. He was warm, burning up. He peeled off his shirt. Kicked off the blankets except for one thin sheet. His mother had given him Benadryl after seeing the spider bites on his hands and neck. He had lied to her, saying he fell asleep in the grass. Woke up with spider bites. He was sure that she believed him. And why not? Ash was not the kind of boy who lied to his parents. Not until recently.

The Benadryl seemed to have helped. The red welts calmed down. He took another dose just now, even though it was only late afternoon. Ash still felt *off* in the same way. Not quite right. What's the thing that people say? I'm not feeling like myself.

Not feeling like myself.

Not feeling like . . .

The book dropped from Ash's hands. His eyes rolled back into his skull. And he slept, and he dreamed, and he flew . . .

◊◊◊

The crow took to the air. Flight felt natural, effortless, free. Up high, the air moved in swirling currents. Waves of air rising and falling like ocean tides. The crow instinctively knew how to ride the currents. Unlike many other birds, the crow did not glide through the air. It continuously flapped its wings.

The crow saw trees and lakes, rivers and grassy meadows. It spied a vast, two-story building below. It swooped down, perching on the top of a pine . . .

In his dream, the boy saw with the eye of the crow and the intelligence of Ash. The building was obscured by trees. Hidden deep in the forest. One primitive logging road, blocked by fallen trees, joined it to the outside world. A small factory of some sort. A research laboratory. A secret place far from prying eyes. The windows have been blacked out.

But the eyes of the crow saw all.

The intelligence of the boy understood.

A great power surged inside the building. Restless, angry. Ash sensed suffering, too. The presence of trapped creatures straining to be free. Outside the building, a chain across the dirt road. A barbwire fence. A helmeted guard with a gun on his hip.

A sign in bold letters that read RESTRICTED AREA: AUTHORIZED PERSONNEL ONLY.

It was a sign the boy had seen before.

In another time. The same place. Todd holding it up for all to see.

And he understood at once that he had traveled back into the past. Through corridors of time . . .

The crow soared again, feeling the rising currents under its wings. Below, time passed. The building flashed brightly. An accident shattered the peace. Sparks flew. A fire raged. Wolves howled. Brick by brick, the building crumbled in fast-forward. Nature reclaimed its ground. The shell of the building collapsed. The ruins covered it up.

Only the concrete, steel, and rebar-reinforced basement rooms remained intact—buried under dross and soil, canopy and roots. The crow saw the motel not far away. The windows to the room. It returned to room 15—where the boy tossed and turned, feverish and chilled . . .

◊◊◊

Another vision. A small pup, weak with hunger. One eye blue, one eye gray. It pauses to lap from a puddle.

Ash felt the ache of hunger in his belly. The aloneness. The fear.

◊◊◊

The boy's eyes shot open. His heart raced, birdlike.

One more piece of the mystery solved.

He did not feel like himself.

Mr. Do entered the room. He held a stack of clean towels. It was dusk. Daisy lay shivering. The old man saw that the dog was unwell. It had caught the sickness. Ash asleep in his bed, fitful and restless.

No peaceful slumber for the sleeper.

The caretaker went to the bathroom and dampened a hand towel with cool water. He carried it to the boy's bedside. Placed it on Ash's forehead. The boy's eyes fluttered. He murmured something. Feverish words. The old man leaned closer to hear. "I flew," the boy said. "I saw a white dog."

He was sweating. Face flushed. Breaking the fever. The old man paused, waited. The boy kicked at the sheet.

Three black feathers fell to the ground.

The old man bent to pick up each feather, one by one. He delicately tucked them into a shirt pocket for safekeeping. Magical objects. A secret he would not share. Mr. Do went to the closet. He came back with a clean, cool, freshly laundered sheet.

Mr. Do removed the old sheet and let it crumple to the floor. He placed the fresh one over the boy. Better, yes. He studied Daisy once more. She barely raised her head. Eyes glassy. *Shhhh*, the old man whispered. Not unkindly. Never unkindly.

"Good dog," the old man said in a soft voice. "Stay."

TWENTY-SEVEN

MONDAY MORNING. Kristoff shuffled across the parking lot in that leaning-forward way of his. Bent at the waist. He wore slippers and a bathrobe and walked with one arm around his stomach. Ash watched him come. He closed the book on his lap, lifted the water bottle from the garden bench, and made room for Kristoff to sit.

Kristoff coughed into the crook of his elbow. His face looked ashen. His hair a tangled mess. That is, he was nearly back to normal. Willow's vampire hottie in navy-blue-striped pajamas. Only two days after they found him at death's door. Kristoff said, "Morning."

Ash returned the greeting.

Kristoff sat beside him. "I noticed you sitting out here."

"Mr. Do's garden. It's my favorite place to read."

"No dog today?"

"No," Ash answered. "She's not well. We're taking her to the vet in town this afternoon. My father has it all mapped out. We seem to be able to go into town, but not any farther. So, yeah, our weird new normal. How are you feeling?"

Kristoff lifted a hand from his knee. Let it drop. "I've been worse."

"You recover quickly," Ash said.

"It's a gift," Kristoff said. "How about you?"

"I've been fighting something," Ash said. "My mother says that spiders have jaws and fangs. Which is freaky if you picture it. Little faces with teeth on the bodies of spiders. When they bite, they inject venom that goes into the blood system. Some spiders are more dangerous than others. The more bites you get, the worse off you are."

Kristoff smiled. "We sound like two old men, swapping stories about our aches and pains."

"One old man, maybe," Ash remarked.

Kristoff nodded, point taken.

They sat together under the morning sun in silence. In no hurry. Ash waited. Honeybees danced among the yellow and purple flowers.

"I owe you an explanation," Kristoff finally said. "And my thanks."

"The wolf led me to you," Ash said. "She was very insistent."

"She can be that way," Kristoff said, grinning. He leaned to the side, lifted a wallet from the side pocket of his bathrobe. He took out a tattered black-and-white photograph. "My mother."

It was a photo of a woman. Fifty years old, maybe. She had Kristoff's bone structure. The cheekbones and chin and haunted eyes. Her gray-and-black hair pulled tightly back. A scar ran from below her right eye, across her nose, to her left cheek.

"She never talks about how she got that scar," Kristoff said. "One day, it was just suddenly there."

Ash sat in the stillness. He felt the blood in his veins, the nerve endings tingling in the tips of his fingers. He had seen the scar before, of course. Across the muzzle of the dire wolf. "Your mother *is* the wolf? But how?"

Kristoff looked off into the distance. He shrugged and shook his head. "Parents. You know how they are."

Ash laughed.

What else could he do but accept the wild crazy of their situation?

"Exit 13 Motel," Kristoff said, gesturing with a flick of the wrist. "A riddle, wrapped in a mystery, inside a puzzle; perhaps there is a key to explain it all."

"How long have you been here?"

Kristoff pursed his lips as if to prevent the words from escaping his mouth. "I see your father heading out in the car most mornings," Kristoff said, changing the subject. "Every day, seeking a way home."

"He stopped," Ash said. "I think he may have given up. I can't decide if that's a good thing or not."

Kristoff tapped his thumb ring against his leg. Engraved with the image of a wolf. "For me, the urge comes and goes. Time passes. I accept my fate. Then one day, I find myself searching in the tunnels. Opening doors that should not be opened. I guess I keep trying, too," he admitted.

"Is that what you were doing out there?"

"There are animals," Kristoff said. "Mistreated, unloved."

"You were holding a puppy."

Kristoff nodded. "I've meant to ask."

"It ran away," Ash said. "I looked away—the tangle of vines—and the puppy was gone."

Kristoff lowered his eyes. He paused, carefully selecting his words. "I believe this world—Exit 13— is wrong. *Somehow it is all wrong.* And the biggest wrong is what has happened to those animals in the Whispering Pines. Something terrible, I don't know what."

"And they need our love," Ash said.

"Yes," Kristoff said. "I think so."

"And will that make this world right again?"

Kristoff gave a resigned shrug. "We can only try."

"You didn't have to travel that far to find a lost animal," Ash said. "There was another reason why you were in the forest. What was it?"

"There's someone I am trying to . . . recover," Kristoff confessed. It was a curious word choice: *recover*. "And now I wonder if that's why you're here.

That maybe *you are the key*." He leaned back and looked at Ash.

"Me?"

"Do you think it's an accident?" Kristoff asked. "Your family just showed up one day? These gifts you seem to possess."

Ash stared at his hands. "Who are you trying to find?"

"My father," Kristoff said. "He's out there somewhere. Alive or dead, I do not know."

"I used to think that you were keeping us here," Ash said. "My father still doesn't trust you."

"Believe me. I have no control over that," Kristoff replied.

"How can I help?"

"I wish I knew. Make it right, suppose." He looked to the sky. A thin line of stratus clouds hung low on the horizon. "Nature isn't in balance here. The laws of physics don't apply. You can feel it in the air. Time, space, the animals . . ."

Kristoff gripped Ash's forearm. "You could help the animals. So many are lost in the woods. Somehow I know that's important. Trying to make that right."

Ash remembered the bent-eared cat. He and Willow rescued it from the woods and found it a home. There was something half dead about it. A smell. Its unnatural, stiff-legged walk. "I have the same feeling. But I don't understand why it would help."

Kristoff picked up a pebble from the ground. Flicked it with his thumb. "Every kindness helps. If we can't believe in that . . . what's left?"

Ash said, "This place has changed me. I can sense things. Hear voices. See in the dark."

"And this is new?"

Ash shrugged. "I have always been different. Separate. But I guess I figured that everyone else felt that way deep down inside. We all saw things that couldn't be explained, heard creatures whispering under the bed."

Kristoff tilted his head to indicate the book on Ash's lap. "Your powers are growing?"

"Yes, I think so."

A crow landed on a fence post. Its black feathers shone in the sun. Probably the same one from the other day. It was hard to tell with crows. "They say that crows are the most intelligent birds," Kristoff observed. "This one seems to spend time alone, away from the roost. A solitary crow. Not common. Some crows even recognize human faces."

"In my dream—I think it was a dream—I saw a building from years ago, back in the woods," Ash confessed. "A research lab or something. It's gone now. But I wonder—"

"What?" Kristoff asked.

"I wonder why it appeared to me. What does it mean?"

Kristoff put a hand on Ash's shoulder. He was still a child, a young boy. Not even twelve. There was so much to learn. Kristoff stood to leave. "I'm glad we talked."

Ash looked up and nodded.

Kristoff said, "I would do anything to see my father again. For one day, one hour. I feel his absence all the time—all the things we never said. That's why I was out there. I keep hoping to make my family whole again."

TWENTY-EIGHT

WILLOW SAT ON THE RUG next to Daisy and watched her dog breathe. She heard a faint wheeze. At one point, Daisy half rose on stiff legs, turned, and plopped down with her head on Willow's lap. She favored her right front paw, refusing to put weight on it. The girl reassuringly ran her hand from the nape of Daisy's neck, along her withers and back, down to the dog's rump.

Just to say, *I'm here.*

Mrs. McGinn knocked and opened the door that connected rooms 15 and 16. Sometimes they kept it open. It made the small rooms feel more spacious, more like a home. But most of the time, the door was kept shut for privacy. "How's our girl?" she asked.

"Daisy or me?" Willow asked.

"Both, I suppose."

"She's not right, Mama," Willow said. She felt warm pressure building up behind her eyes. "Can't we bring her in now?"

"Sweetie, we got the earliest appointment possible. They worked hard to fit us in," Mrs. McGinn said. "Everyone is doing their best."

Willow looked down, unsatisfied.

Daisy did not stir.

"I'll leave you two alone," Willow's mother said. "Can I get you anything?"

"Twizzlers."

"Will, please, we just had breakfast."

"Dots, then?"

"You inherited your father's sweet tooth," Mrs. McGinn said.

"I'm fine, Mama," Willow said, even though she wasn't fine at all. *Fine* was a distant island—miles away. Meanwhile, Willow drowned in a bottomless sea. The door shut.

Willow pulled out her phone and tapped at the keys.

> **Willow: My dog is sick. Did you know I have a dog? Daisy. She's a goldendoodle. The sweetest dog ever. Gentle and snuggly. She doesn't have a mean bone in her body. We got her when I was five. My dad says that pets are built-in heartache. I don't know about that. I had two goldfish that died. I won them at a ring toss at a school fair. We flushed them down the toilet. I think I read a poem or something at their memorial service. Then I went outside to play. It wasn't real heartbreaking. I don't know. I just can't get too wrapped up in a fish, you know what I'm saying?**

She waited, no response. It had been two days. Ever since that day with Hoover. All that running. The confusion of doors.

Willow: You saved my life, you know. I mean, I don't think Hoover was going to hurt me or anything. But puke, what a bully! What happened to him, do you know? And, okay, I know you don't want to tell me, but WHO ARE YOU???!!! How do you know all the things? It feels like you are an angel or something. Our UFO friends are leaving today. For a bunch of whackjobs, they were really nice and funny and only half crazy. I guess it will get quiet around here again. Kristoff is getting better. I'm sooooo glad about that. But right now, I'm just scared for Daisy. I don't want to lose my good sweet dog. Sigh. Your friend, Willow McGinn.

Willow's phone buzzed.

A.F.: Good luck with your good sweet dog.
A.F.: Did you not figure out my name yet?

Figured out the name? Willow hadn't "figured" anything. So she considered it once again. A.F.

Willow: Just tell me.

A.F.: The initials stand for A Friend.

So there it was.

A stranger.

And a friend.

TWENTY-NINE

VELMA STEPPED OUT of the motel room. She was wearing red running shorts, sneakers, a new ALIENS RULE! T-shirt, and orange socks that climbed halfway up her calves (of course). Todd carried luggage out to the van.

"You leaving already?" Ash asked.

"I'm going for a run first," Velma said. "A shower, coffee, and we're gone."

"How did the costume contest go?"

Todd laughed. "She won first prize! Was there ever any doubt?"

"Congratulations," Ash said.

Velma grinned. "Jinkies! What can I say?"

Ash gestured toward his room. "Don't leave without saying goodbye."

"Sure thing, kid," Todd said. "And you know, we had a great time at the UFO Fest and everything. Lot of mind-boggling information. Deep stuff. But that trip in the woods with you? Man, that was bananas. I'm not going to forget that for as long as I live."

Ash found his father sitting by the firepit. It wasn't lit. He was just staring into the charred remains of gray-white ashes. Elbows on his knees, chin in his hands.

"You okay, Dad?"

Mr. McGinn turned to his son in surprise. "What? Oh, yeah. Just lost in thought. How you doing, buddy?"

Ash shrugged. "What were you thinking about?"

Mr. McGinn sighed and looked at his son. "You know, same old thing."

"It's not your fault," Ash said.

"I keep trying to think where I went wrong. What I can do to get us out of this mess."

"Maybe," Ash said, "we're here for a reason?"

His father lifted his head and looked around. They

were alone. He pulled his chair closer to Ash. "You know, I used to read a lot of ghost stories as a kid. Anything scary, I was all in. There's always one question with any ghost. *Why is it sticking around?* Why not go on to the next phase or . . . whatever, you know? And the answer is always the same. There is something left for it to do. A task to complete. Maybe that's why we're here. If we ever hope to depart, we first need to finish the job."

"I didn't know that—about you and the ghost stories," Ash said.

"Oh, yeah. From Edgar Allan Poe to Stephen King, I read 'em all."

"I heard a joke," Ash said. "It's pretty bad."

"I like bad jokes."

"That's because you're a dad," Ash said with a smile. "All dads like bad jokes. Especially with puns."

Mr. McGinn smiled. "It's part of the job description. Dads are required to like bad jokes. Let's hear it."

"What do you call someone with no body and no nose?"

Mr. McGinn's eyes twinkled. "Nobody knows.

"You heard it before?"

"I've heard them all," Ash's father said. "Sometimes I think there aren't new ones anymore."

Ash saw movement across the lawn. The great wolf stepped out of the forest. Kristoff's mother. She stood still, proud, and strong. Stared directly at Ash. Mr. McGinn followed his son's gaze. "A friend of yours?" he asked.

Ash was startled. "What?"

"The wolf."

"You see it, too?"

"You thought you were the only one?" Mr. McGinn asked.

"Yes," Ash replied. "I did."

The father placed a hand on his son's shoulder. "You are not alone, Ash. You are not the only one. But I never wanted this for you."

Ash looked at his father in confusion.

"Look, Ash," Mr. McGinn said. "All these years, I never told you. But I always knew you weren't like the other kids in the neighborhood. Different even from Willow. Different from Mom. And it's my fault, all of it. I always saw something of myself in you."

"You?"

"Don't look so unhappy," Mr. McGinn said, smiling. "I am your father, after all. You have my DNA. Scientists call them 'shadow traits.' Characteristics in the parent carried forward in the child. I don't have it nearly as strong as you do, but I guess the seeds were in me. Passed down to you."

Ash watched as a single tear rolled down his father's face.

"I'm sorry, son."

"It's okay, Dad. I'm glad," Ash said. "I'm proud to be like you."

Mr. McGinn shook his head. "It won't be easy. Hearing voices, seeing things. Feeling different from everyone else."

"Maybe it's a gift," Ash said.

"Maybe," his father agreed uncertainly.

"Does Mom know?"

Mr. McGinn glanced in the direction of the motel rooms. He smiled. "I tell your mother everything."

Ash rose from his chair. He stared at the dire wolf—Kristoff's mother—who seemed to be waiting for him. "Do you mind if I . . . ?"

"Is it safe?"

"Yes," Ash replied.

"We're leaving for the vet in an hour. Be sure you're ready." Mr. McGinn raised a hand, signaling for Ash to wait for one final comment. "And take it from me: If any trees talk to you, you don't *have to* talk back."

He laughed for the first time in a week.

"Thanks, Dad." Ash paused for a moment, standing beside his seated father. It felt good to talk about things. Even hard things. Ash reached down and wrapped his arms around his father, awkwardly hugging his neck and shoulders.

"I love you, Dad," he said.

And then he left to see what that wolf wanted now.

THIRTY

WHAT DOES THE WOLF WANT?

That was the million-dollar question. It was the wolf that first led Ash into the woods on the night of their arrival. That led him to the Unnumbered Room. That howled through the night when Kristoff was missing.

Now Ash followed the wolf—Kristoff's mother!—to where the woods bordered the back of the motel. "I can't go in there," Ash said. "I'm sorry, I'm just not ready for that."

The wolf sat.

Ash sat beside it.

Shoulder to shoulder.

The wolf rose, paced the edge of the woods, whining softly. Back and forth, back and forth. At last, a nose poked through. The head of a dog. It was skittish, hesitant, and frightened. It came all the way out of the woods and stopped there. Not a step closer.

Ash leaned forward on his hands. "Come on," he whispered. "We met before. Remember? I'm not going to hurt you."

The dog lowered its head, unwilling to look directly at Ash. It was some kind of hound. Floppy ears. Long legs. Tan body with a white chest, black all around the mouth. It dropped to the ground, scratching vigorously at its ears with its back leg. Fleas and ticks, probably. Ash saw that it was undernourished. Patches of fur had fallen out. Scratches and scabs on its body.

Still on his hands and knees, Ash crawled forward. The dog went into high alert.

"It's okay," Ash whispered.

He moved forward another foot.

The dog disappeared into the woods.

"I'll be right back," Ash told the forest. The wolf sat sphinxlike, vigilant. It would wait.

Back in room 15, Willow was still seated on the floor beside Daisy. She was reading Ash's book, a chapter titled "The Art of Self-Defense."

"How's Daisy doing?" Ash asked as he entered the room.

"Not good," Willow answered. "Sleeping mostly. Her front paw is tender to the touch. Maybe something's broken."

Ash nodded distractedly. They kept food supplies in a cooler. Mostly quick snacks and liquids. He slathered a piece of bread with peanut butter. He took two of Daisy's biscuits and crumpled them over the peanut butter.

"What the heck are you doing, LB?" Willow asked.

Ash topped it off with a second piece of bread. The sandwich was complete. He looked around the room. "Do we have any rope?"

"Ash? What's going on?"

"Come and you'll see," Ash replied. "I could use your help."

Willow looked down at Daisy. The sweet dog was sleeping quietly. Willow kissed Daisy on her cheek. "Love is love is love," she whispered.

160

Ash stood at the door, tapping his foot impatiently. He held a coil of rope that his mother used as a clothesline. The doggy-treat sandwich was in his other hand. "Let's go, Will."

She filled a bowl with water and followed him out the door.

When Ash and Willow came around the building, the wolf retreated.

Ash tore off pieces of sandwich. He laid them out in a line like Elliott from *E.T.* coaxing the alien out with Reese's Pieces. It was a great idea and Ash didn't mind stealing it.

"What now?" Willow asked.

"We sit quietly—and hope," Ash answered.

After a few minutes, the nose poked through. Nervous, uncertain, and afraid. But the animal's hunger overrode its fears. It gobbled up the first piece of sandwich. Smacked its mouth with its tongue, tasting the peanut butter. It inched closer. Stretched out its neck as far as possible . . . and gobbled down another piece of bread.

Ash and Willow sat in perfect stillness. Willow began to speak in a mellow stream of words, burbling like a river. "That's good . . . there you go . . . nice and easy . . . come and share our water . . . so fresh and cold."

And finally the dog drank from the bowl, lapping thirstily.

Willow reached out her hand for the dog to sniff. She placed the coiled rope over its head. Gently, softly, and slowly. "Poor thing is trembling," she said.

"I can't imagine what it's been through," Ash said. "All those bug bites."

"I'm so sorry that you've suffered," Willow told the ragged, flea-ridden dog. "That's over now. Things will be better soon. You'll see."

As if it understood, the dog—with food in its belly for the first time in days—licked Willow on the hand.

THIRTY-ONE

A CROWD OF DEPARTING guests milled around the parking lot. Two carloads of people were ready to head out: Todd, Joris, Velma, and Ren in the van; three others in a Honda: Sash, Darwin, and Monica.

"There you are," Joris said. "I was hoping we'd see you kids before we left."

Ren saw the sensitive, long-legged pup attached to the rope in Willow's hand. "Wait, is that the dog from before?"

Willow and Ash told them about the rescue.

"Poor thing, he looks frightened," Ren said. "Who knows. It may not have been near humans for a long time."

"Whoa, that's a black mouth cur!" Sash exclaimed. "I grew up with a dog just like that."

"That's the name of the breed? Black mouth cur?" Monica asked.

"Don't look at me, I didn't come up with the name," Sash said. "Sweet breed, though. It'll hunt, protect the house, good with kids."

"Kids?" Monica asked warily.

Sash blushed, rosy patches above his massive beard.

Ash explained that they couldn't keep it.

"I wish I could adopt it," Ren said. "A rescue dog like this needs a lot of attention. Time to adjust. It has to learn how to trust people again. But I'm maxed out with a mastiff at home."

"I guess we'll have to take it to the pound," Willow said, making her saddest face. The dog stayed pressed to her side, slightly behind her legs. Shy and sensitive, it trembled. Willow aimed her words like an arrow directly at Sash. "Is it true? You really had one of these when you were a kid?"

She watched the big, bearded man's heart slowly melt.

He squatted down near the dog. It pulled away.

Timid and nervous. Sash didn't reach out for the dog. He waited, speaking softly, for it to come forward.

"I don't know. He looks damaged," Joris pointed out. "Unhealthy, skittish. You don't have any idea what he's been through."

Sash shook his head. "This dog just needs love, patience, space—and a safe place to live. That's the beauty of a rescue dog. It's a way to really make a difference in the world." He slowly reached out an open hand. The dog sniffed it, whimpered softly. After another minute, the dog tentatively rubbed his head against Sash's forearm.

"What do you think?" Sash asked Monica.

She smiled and nodded her head.

"Are you sure it's okay? I can take it?" Sash asked Ash and Willow.

"It needs to get to a vet," Willow said. "He's probably been living in the woods for a while."

"My friend is a vet," Sash said. "I'll call her right when I get home."

"In the meantime, we can stop in town," Monica offered. "Buy some flea and tick spray, a new leash and collar—"

"Treats—" Sash added.

"And a toy," Darwin said.

"And don't forget love," Willow said. "That's free. Lots and lots of love."

"One rule, Sash," Monica said. "You are sitting in the back with that dog. I am not touching it until we get rid of those fleas."

"Awesome, I ride shotgun!" Darwin pumped his fist and laughed. *Hee-hee, hee-haw, hee-hee.*

It reminded Ash that he had one more thing to settle. Ash moved to Darwin's side and spoke in a quiet voice. "It was you that night, by the pool."

Darwin grinned. "Yeah, that was me. I slept out there every night under the stars. It's my happy place."

"You scared me. Calling out in the dark like that."

"Sorry, I didn't mean to frighten you," Darwin apologized. "What were you doing sneaking around in the middle of the night, anyway?"

"Sleepwalking," Ash answered.

"Hey, Ash," Sash called. "I need you and Willow to come in for a photo, please. Monica, can you take it? I want to remember the day I first met Scooby."

"Scooby?" Velma asked, laughing. "Are you seriously going to name your dog after a cartoon?"

"Sure am," Sash replied. "Scooby Dooby Doo!"

Monica snapped the photo. Scooby and Sash—with the grinning man's arm around Ash's shoulder.

Joris held out a hand. Ash shook it. "Be careful around those liminal spaces," he joked.

"Sure thing," Ash promised.

A tow truck rattled into the lot. Mr. Do walked out of the office, waving a greeting to the driver. He directed the truck to a car that had been abandoned by a guest. Willow saw that it was Mr. Hoover's car with darkened windows. In minutes, Hoover's car was winched up and towed away. The last trace of the man in room 6.

At least, she hoped.

Even if Hoover was gone for good, Willow wondered if that was the last they'd hear from X-Star Corp. Somehow she doubted it. They'd be back. Send someone else. A minute later, Monica, Sash, and Darwin were waving goodbye from the car. Sash cracked open the back window. Scooby sat beside him, pressed close together. Darwin cranked up the

tunes. "Space Oddity" by David Bowie. Figured.

After goodbyes, Velma, Joris, and Ren climbed into the van. Todd gave the horn a friendly toot. He lowered the driver's side window and called out, "We'll be back next year for the second annual UFO Fest—Velma has to defend her crown!"

They drove away.

Down the driveway and gone.

Ash and Willow waited a minute.

Another minute.

And another.

"I guess they got away," Willow said. "They aren't trapped here."

"That means there's hope," Ash replied.

Their parents came outside from room 16. "Kids, gather up Daisy!" Mrs. McGinn announced. "It's time for our appointment with the vet."

THIRTY-TWO

THE VET WAS A THIN, short man named Dr. Sayad. He wore a white lab coat and a pair of glasses perched on the top of his head. The entire family crowded into the examination room. Daisy was so tired and weak, she didn't protest as the doctor checked her out on the stainless-steel table. Daisy protested softly when he probed her front right paw. "Sweet dog," Dr. Sayad said. "You are not feeling well, are you?"

"I was wondering if she got a tick bite?" Mrs. McGinn said.

"We'll need to draw some blood—it won't hurt—and we'll know the results by tomorrow," Dr. Sayad said. "I am a little concerned by her front paw. It's infected. Fortunately there are no broken bones. Perhaps we'll take an X-ray to be on the safe side."

"Yes, of course," Mrs. McGinn answered. When it came to anything medical, she always stepped forward as the voice of the family.

"I would like to start her off with a heavy dose of antibiotics right away," Dr. Sayad said.

"Whatever you think is necessary," said Mrs. McGinn.

The doctor studied Daisy's injured paw. "Hmmm." He paused. "Interesting. She was bitten."

"Like a tick or . . . ?"

"No, I don't think so. I see two clear markings. A snake, perhaps? Though that's extremely unusual around here. Where did she get bitten?"

"On the leg," Ash said.

The doctor smiled. "Yes. I meant, where was Daisy?"

Mrs. McGinn looked at Ash and Willow. "Well?"

"We were in the woods behind the motel," Ash admitted.

Dr. Sayad's eyebrows arched. He looked from Ash

to his parents. "We're staying at the Exit 13 Motel—"
Mr. McGinn said.

"Temporarily," Mrs. McGinn added.

The doctor didn't comment right away. Just nodded
once. He patted his pockets absentmindedly. Then the
top of his head—there they were—his reading glasses.
Finally he said, "That's probably not a safe place for
Daisy."

"We understand," Mrs. McGinn answered.

"The good news is that Daisy should be fine within
a few days," the doctor said. "She'll need a full course
of antibiotics for at least ten days. Plenty of rest. And
please, keep her out of those woods. In fact," he said,
"I don't think anyone should be walking around in
the Whispering Pines. I've heard stories."

Twenty minutes later, everyone was feeling encour-
aged. Mr. McGinn carried Daisy into the back seat.
Ash and Willow sat sandwiched beside her.

"Well, I'm so relieved," Mrs. McGinn announced
from the front seat. "If the doctor's correct, Daisy will
be feeling much better in a day or two."

Mr. McGinn drove through the heart of town. It
looked pretty. Stores and shops with big, open sidewalks

for people to walk around. Nice houses, too. "I've been thinking," Mrs. McGinn said. "I'd like to make jewelry again. I used to make beautiful jewelry and then I stopped."

"You got busy," her husband said, reaching out a hand.

"I could even sell it," she said. "Create a website."

"Maybe you should wait until—"

"No," she said to her husband. "I don't want to wait. This feels like the right time for me. I could use a project."

The car came to an intersection. The motel was down the road to the left. A right turn would lead back to the highway. And maybe, just maybe, an escape. It was worth a try.

Mr. McGinn hesitated before putting on the blinker.

"Hey, Dad," Ash said. "I'm pretty sure Daisy is a genius."

"What's that?" he replied, still staring down the beckoning road.

"Yeah, for real," Ash continued. "I asked her what's two minus two and she said nothing."

Willow groaned.

Mr. McGinn laughed and said, "Good one!"

He looked at his children in the rearview mirror. He turned to his wife. "Tell you what. Maybe we should get some pizza and eat it back at the motel. What do you guys think? Ready to go home?"

Everyone agreed that was a good idea.

Some pizza and then home.

At least, home for now.

Exit 13 Motel.

THIRTY-THREE

NICE WORK, WILL.

YEAH, SWEET. THANKS FOR LENDING ME THAT BOOK, LB.

THIRTY-FOUR

WILLOW PUSHED THE CART along the row of rooms. The motel wasn't as busy as it had been a few weeks ago. Fortunately, Kristoff kept her on for part-time work. It wasn't much, but it was something to do. Willow enjoyed keeping busy and it gave her an excuse to visit with the vampire hottie. She knew that Kristoff was too old for her, *hee-hee*, but he still gave her goose bumps (in a good way). Ash helped out in Mr. Do's garden. He was also learning how to paint—starting on the trim of the motel. Today, Willow had to clean one room that had been vacated—and double-check that room 8 was all set. A guest with a large dog was scheduled to arrive that afternoon.

Willow was putting the supplies away when a large, long, black sedan eased up to the office. A tall woman stepped out. She wore a fashionable black dress with a bold white stripe running diagonally across it. Red high heels matched her red lipstick. Though she did not look old, the woman's hair was perfectly white and flowed loosely over her shoulders. Her posture was perfect, like a ballerina. The woman gracefully opened the back door and out stepped a massive dog. Willow recognized the breed as an Irish wolfhound. It was calm and dignified—a perfect complement to the elegant woman on the other end of the leather leash.

The woman wore a red-and-black hat with the brim pulled low, concealing her eyes. A spray of black feathers grew out the back of it.

The woman paused when she spotted Willow observing their arrival.

As if remembering a forgotten detail, she pulled out her phone.

Tap, tap, tap. Her thumbs danced quickly over the keys.

Willow's pocket vibrated.

Heart beating faster, Willow reached for the message on her phone.

> **A.F.: It's lovely to finally see you in person. Don't you agree? Perhaps there are more adventures to come? We can certainly hope so!**

Willow looked up, confused.

Could this be?

The woman, a friend, offered a gracious nod as if in response to Willow's unspoken question. Yes, yes, yes. She offered a bemused smile. Willow's mysterious friend gave the wolfhound a gentle tug, said, "Come, Sebastian," and stepped into the office.

THE END

ABOUT THE AUTHOR

James Preller is the author of many popular books for young readers, including the Jigsaw Jones and Scary Tales series. He's also written award-winning middle-grade fiction, including *Six Innings*, *Bystander*, *Blood Mountain*, and more. He lives in Delmar, New York, with his wife, Lisa. He has three children: Nicholas, Gavin, and Maggie—and Echo, a rescue dog from Kentucky. James maintains an active blog at jamespreller.com and very much enjoys school visits.

ABOUT THE ILLUSTRATOR

For much longer than he can reliably remember, Kevin Keele has enjoyed drawing. His art has been featured in numerous picture books, magazines, and board and card games, many of which are bestsellers and award winners. He's a game developer by day and an illustrator by night (technically, early mornings since, as he's gotten older, he's lost all ability to stay up past 10:00 p.m.). He lives in Utah with his wife and three sons. They're the caretakers of one cat, three chickens, and thousands of honeybees.

BE SURE NOT TO MISS THE FIRST BOOK IN THE

EXIT 13 SERIES:

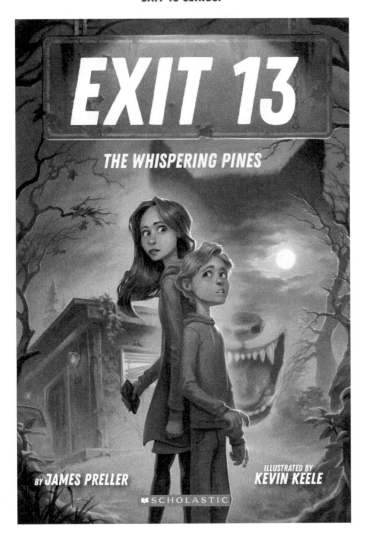